"A wildly entertaining mix of action a[nd] humor and a bizarre love story, this ... done right, science fiction can be one of the most entertaining genres out there. Between fighting alien creatures, pondering what it means to be human, and looking at cloning from various perspectives, there is something for everyone here, and Ashton delivers all of it with plenty of wittiness and flair."

—NPR (Best Books of 2022)

"The fun [in reading *Mickey7*] is trying to keep up with Mr. Ashton's twists and turns, and the extra fun is that you never do."

—*The Wall Street Journal*

"*Mickey7* is a smart philosophical satire masquerading as an adventure novel. It draws readers in with flippant black humor and a clever premise, then stabs them in the back with devastating insight into the human talent for suppressing intolerable truths."

—*New York Journal of Books*

"Sci-fi readers will be drawn in by the inventive premise and stick around for the plucky narrator."

—*Publishers Weekly*

"Ashton's novel begins as farce and ends as something considerably deeper; as an Expendable, Mickey7 is able to ask what makes someone human or who has the right to destroy a place in order to occupy it. Highly recommended for readers of colonization SF."

—*Library Journal* (starred review)

"A multilayered, wildly entertaining story . . . Ashton is a talented storyteller and *Mickey7* has something for everyone while also putting a fresh spin on the idea of clones."

—*Locus*

"A sharp speculative work that is both intellectually oriented and action-packed. [*Mickey7*] is smart and funny and well crafted across the board. If you're a fan of science fiction, you won't regret meeting Mickey. He's so fine."   —*The Maine Edge*

"A killer premise, and its mix of social commentary, dark humor, and horrifying surprises makes it ideal for the director of *Parasite*."
—*The Film Stage*

"*Mickey7* is a unique blend of thought-provoking sci-fi concepts, farcical relationship drama, and exotic body horror. Edward Ashton keeps it all grounded via a protagonist who experiences the wonders of interstellar travel and alien contact while literally having the worst job in the universe. The result is alternately amusing, intriguing, and horrifying, with each chapter seeming to engage a different part of your brain."   —Jason Pargin, *New York Times* bestselling author of *John Dies at the End*

"Fun, thoughtful, and immensely personable, *Mickey7* is a brisk, spirited sci-fi romp with alien intelligences, extra lives, and a little romance, too. Hugely enjoyable."
—Max Barry, author of *Providence*

"*Mickey7* is a mind-bending and powerful exploration of identity. This is why we read science fiction! Highly recommended."
—Jonathan Maberry, *New York Times* bestselling author of *Rage* and *Ink*

"I loved *Mickey7*—a smart, breezy SF novel that doubles as a pitch-black comedy of errors."   —Dexter Palmer, critically acclaimed author of *Version Control*

"Andy Weir, watch out!"   —Stephen Baxter, author of *Time*

ALSO BY EDWARD ASHTON

Three Days in April

The End of Ordinary

Edward Ashton

ST. MARTIN'S GRIFFIN
NEW YORK

Published in the United States by St. Martin's Griffin, an imprint of St. Martin's Publishing Group

MICKEY7. Copyright © 2022 by Edward Ashton. All rights reserved. Printed in the United States of America. For information, address St. Martin's Publishing Group, 120 Broadway, New York, NY 10271.

www.stmartins.com

The Library of Congress has cataloged the hardcover edition as follows:

Names: Ashton, Edward (Science fiction writer), author.
Title: Mickey7 / Edward Ashton.
Description: First edition. | New York : St. Martin's Press, 2022.
Identifiers: LCCN 2021042263 | ISBN 9781250275035 (hardcover) |
    ISBN 9781250275042 (ebook)
Subjects: LCGFT: Science fiction.
Classification: LCC PS3601.S567 M53 2022 | DDC 813/.6—dc23
LC record available at https://lccn.loc.gov/2021042263

ISBN 978-1-250-87528-0 (trade paperback)

Our books may be purchased in bulk for promotional, educational, or business use. Please contact your local bookseller or the Macmillan Corporate and Premium Sales Department at 1-800-221-7945, extension 5442, or by email at MacmillanSpecialMarkets@macmillan.com.

First St. Martin's Griffin Edition: 2023

10 9 8 7 6 5 4 3

For Jen. If you hadn't ended civilization, none of this would have happened.

THIS IS GONNA be my stupidest death ever.

It's just past 26:00, and I'm sprawled on my back on a rough stone floor, in a darkness so black that I may as well be blind. My ocular wastes a long five seconds hunting for stray visible-spectrum photons before finally giving up and flipping over to infrared. There's still not much to see, but at least I can make out the roof of the chamber above me, glowing now in a pale, spectral gray, and the black ring of the ice-crusted opening that must have brought me here.

Question: What the hell happened?

The last few minutes of my memory are fragmentary—mostly unconnected images and snippets of sound. I remember Berto dropping me off at the head of the crevasse. I remember climbing down along a broken jumble of ice blocks. I remember walking. I remember looking up, seeing a boulder jutting out of the ice about thirty meters up the south wall. It looked a little like a monkey's head. I remember smiling, and then . . .

. . . and then there was nothing under my left foot, and I was falling.

Son of a bitch. I wasn't looking where I was going. I was staring up at that stupid monkey-head rock, thinking about how I'd describe it to Nasha when I got back to the dome, and I stepped into a hole.

Stupidest. Death. Ever.

A shiver runs the length of my body. The cold was bad enough up top, when I was moving. Down here, though, pressed against the bedrock, it's soaking into me, eating through the skin suit and the two layers of thermals, seeping down through hair and skin and muscle and all the way into my bones. I shiver again, and a sudden jolt of pain runs from my left wrist up to my shoulder. I look down. There's a bulge where there shouldn't be one, pressing against the fabric just at the point where my glove meets the sleeve of my outer thermal. I start to pull off the glove, thinking that maybe the cold will help keep the swelling down, but another jolt of pain stops that experiment almost before it's started. Even just trying to make a fist, the pain ramps up from bad to blinding as soon as my fingers start to curl.

Must have banged it on something during the fall. Broken? Maybe. Sprained? Definitely.

Pain means I'm still alive, right?

I sit up slowly, shake my head clear, and blink to a comm window. I'm too far out to pick up any of the colony repeaters, but Berto must still be close, because I'm getting just a hint of a signal. Not enough for voice or video, but I can probably manage text. My eye flickers to the keyboard icon, and it expands to fill a quarter of my field of view.

\<Mickey7\>: Berto. You getting this?
\<RedHawk\>: Affirmative. Still alive, huh?
\<Mickey7\>: So far. I'm stuck, though.

\<RedHawk\>: No kidding. I saw what happened. You walked right into a hole.

\<Mickey7\>: Yeah, I figured that out.

\<RedHawk\>: Not a little hole, Mickey. A big one. What the hell, buddy?

\<Mickey7\>:I was looking at a rock.

\<RedHawk\>:...

\<Mickey7\>: It looked like a monkey.

\<RedHawk\>: Stupidest death ever.

\<Mickey7\>: Yeah, well, only if I die, right? Speaking of which, any chance you're coming for me?

\<RedHawk\>: Uh ...

\<RedHawk\>: No.

\<Mickey7\>: Seriously?

\<RedHawk\>: Seriously.

\<Mickey7\>:...

\<Mickey7\>: Why not?

\<RedHawk\>: Well, mostly because I'm hovering two hundred meters over the spot where you went down right now, and I'm still barely reading you. You're deep underground, my friend, and we are definitely in creeper territory. It would take a hell of an effort and a great deal of personal risk to get you back out—and I can't justify that kind of risk for an Expendable, you know?

\<Mickey7\>: Oh. Right.

\<Mickey7\>: Not for a friend either, huh?

\<RedHawk\>: Come on, Mickey. That's a cheap shot. It's not like you're really dying or anything. I'll file a loss report on you when I get back to the dome. This is line of duty. There's no way Marshall won't approve your regen. You'll be out of the tank and back in your bed tomorrow.

\<Mickey7\>: Oh, that's great. I mean, I'm sure that'll be convenient for you. But in the meantime, I have to die in a hole.

\<RedHawk\>: Yeah, that sucks.

<Mickey7>:That sucks? Really? That's all you've got?

<RedHawk>:I'm sorry, Mickey, but what do you want? I feel bad that
    you're about to die down there, but seriously, this is your job, right?

<Mickey7>:I'm not even current, you know. I haven't uploaded in over
    a month.

<RedHawk>:That . . . is not my fault. Don't worry, though. I'll fill you in
    on what you've been up to. Got any private stuff you've done since
    your last upload that you think you might need to know?

<Mickey7>:Um . . .

<Mickey7>:No, I guess not.

<RedHawk>:Perfect. Then we're all set.

<Mickey7>: . . .

<RedHawk>:All good, Mickey?

<Mickey7>:Yeah. All good. Thanks a lot, Berto.

I blink away from the window, lean back against the rock wall,
and close my eyes. I can't believe that chickenshit bastard's not
coming for me.

Oh, who am I kidding? I can totally believe it.

So, what next? Sit here and wait to die? I have no idea how
far I tumbled down that bore hole or drop shaft or whatever it
was before I hit ground in this . . . whatever this is. It might have
been twenty meters. From the way Berto was talking, it might
have been more like a hundred. The opening I dropped through
is right there, no more than three meters up. Even if I could reach
it, though, there's no way I'm climbing with this wrist.

In my line of work, you spend a lot of time pondering different
ways to die—when you're not actually experiencing them, that
is. I've never frozen to death before. I've definitely thought about
it, though. It's been hard not to since we made landfall on this
godforsaken ball of ice. It should be pretty easy, relatively speaking. You get chilly, fall asleep, and then don't wake up, right? I'm

starting to drift, thinking that at least maybe this won't be such a bad way to go, when my ocular pings. I blink to answer.

<Black Hornet>: Hey babe.
<Mickey7>: Hey Nasha. What can I do for you?
<Black Hornet>: Just sit tight. I'm in the air, ETA two minutes.
<Mickey7>: Berto pinged you?
<Black Hornet>: Yeah. He doesn't think you're retrievable.
<Mickey7>: But?
<Black Hornet>: He's just not properly motivated.

You know, hope is a funny thing. Thirty seconds ago I was one hundred percent sure I was about to die, and I wasn't really afraid. Now, though, my heart is pounding in my ears and I find myself running down a checklist of everything that could go wrong if Nasha actually manages to get her lifter on the ground up there and makes a rescue attempt. Is the floor of the crevasse even wide enough for her to set down? If it is, will she be able to locate me? If she does, will she have enough cable to reach me?

If she does, what are the chances that all that activity brings the creepers down on her?

Shit.

Shit shit shit.

I can't let her do it.

<Mickey7>: Nasha?
<Black Hornet>: Yeah?
<Mickey7>: Berto's right. I'm not retrievable.
<Black Hornet>:…
<Mickey7>: Nasha?
<Black Hornet>: You sure about this, babe?

I close my eyes again, and breathe in, breathe out. It's just a trip to the tank, right?

<Mickey7>:Yeah, I'm sure. I'm buried deep here, and I'm pretty badly banged up. Honestly, even if you managed to get me back, they'd probably wind up scrapping me anyway.

<Black Hornet>:...

<Black Hornet>:Okay, Mickey. This is your call.

<Black Hornet>:You know I would have come for you, right?

<Mickey7>:Yeah, Nasha. I know.

She goes silent, and I sit there watching her signal strength rising and falling. She's orbiting the drop site. She's trying to triangulate my signal, trying to pin down my location.

I need to end this.

<Mickey7>:Go home, Nasha. I'm checking out now.

<Black Hornet>:Oh.

<Black Hornet>:Okay.

<Black Hornet>:How're you gonna do it?

<Mickey7>:Do what?

<Black Hornet>:Shut down, Mickey. I don't want you going out like Five did. You got a weapon?

<Mickey7>:Nope. Lost my burner on the way down. Honestly, I don't think I'd want to use one of those things on myself anyway. I guess it would be quick, but...

<Black Hornet>:Yeah, that's probably a good call. How about a knife? Or an ice ax?

<Mickey7>:No, and no. And what exactly are you expecting me to do with an ice ax?

<Black Hornet>:I don't know. They're sharp, right? Maybe you could chop yourself in the head or something.

\<Mickey7\>: Look, Nasha, I know you're trying to be helpful, but—

\<Black Hornet\>: You could just pop the seals on your rebreather. Not sure if the low O2 or the high CO would get you first, but either way it shouldn't take more than a few minutes.

\<Mickey7\>: Yeah. I know I haven't tried it, but somehow I don't think slow suffocation is my thing.

\<Black Hornet\>: So what're you gonna do?

\<Mickey7\>: Freeze to death, I guess.

\<Black Hornet\>: Yeah, that works. Peaceful, right?

\<Mickey7\>:I hope so.

Her signal dwindles almost to nothing, then hovers just above zero. She must be hanging just at the edge of transmission range.

\<Black Hornet\>: Hey. You're backed up, right?

\<Mickey7\>: Not for the last six weeks.

\<Black Hornet\>: Why haven't you been uploading?

I really don't want to get into that particular question right now.

\<Mickey7\>: Just lazy, I guess.

\<Black Hornet\>:...

\<Black Hornet\>: I'm sorry about this, babe. I really am.

\<Black Hornet\>: Want me to stay on the line with you?

\<Mickey7\>: No. This might take a while, and if you go down out there, you don't get to come back, remember? You should get back to the dome.

\<Black Hornet\>: You sure?

\<Mickey7\>: Yeah, I'm sure.

\<Black Hornet\>: Love you, babe. When I see you tomorrow, I'll let you know that you went down like a pro tonight.

<Mickey7>: Thanks, Nasha. Love you too.
<Black Hornet>: Goodbye, Mickey.

I blink the window closed, and watch as Nasha's comm signal dwindles the rest of the way down to zero. Berto's already long out of range. I look up. The opening is staring down at me like the devil's anus, and, backed up or not, I'm suddenly not cool with dying. I give my head another shake, and climb to my feet.

HERE'S A THOUGHT experiment for you: Imagine you found out that when you go to sleep at night, you don't just go to sleep. You die. You die, and someone else wakes up in your place the next morning. He's got all your memories. He's got all your hopes and dreams and fears and wishes. He thinks he's you, and all your friends and loved ones do too. He's not you, though, and you're not the guy who went to sleep the night before. You've only existed since this morning, and you will cease to exist when you close your eyes tonight. Ask yourself—would it make any practical difference in your life? Is there any way that you could even tell?

Replace "go to sleep" with "get crushed, or vaporized, or set on fire" and you've pretty much got my life. Trouble in the reactor core? I'm on it. Need to test a sketchy new vaccine? I'm your guy. Need to know if the bathtub absinthe you cooked up is poisonous? I'll get a glass, you bastards. If I die, you can always make another me.

The upside of all that dying is that I really am a shitty kind of immortal. I don't just remember what Mickey1 did. I remember being him. Well, all but the last few minutes of being him, anyway. He—I—died after a hull breach during transit. Mickey2 woke up a few hours later, sure as shit that he was thirty-one years old and had been born back on Midgard. And who knows?

Maybe he was. Maybe that was the original Mickey Barnes looking out through his eyes. How could you tell? And maybe if I
lie down on the floor of this cavern, close my eyes, and pop my
seals, I'll wake up tomorrow morning as Mickey8.

Somehow, though, I doubt it.

Nasha and Berto might not be able to tell the difference, but
deep down on some level below reason, I'm pretty sure I'd know
I was dead.

THERE'S PRETTY MUCH nothing in the way of visible-range photons down here, but my ocular is picking up just enough in the
shortwave infrared to get a look around. As it turns out, there
are a half dozen tunnels leading out of this chamber. All of them
slope downward.

That shouldn't be.

None of this should be, actually.

The tunnels look like lava tubes, but according to the orbital
survey, there isn't supposed to be any volcanism within a thousand kilometers of here. That's one of the reasons we picked this
place for our first base camp, even though it's far enough off
the equator that the crappy climate of this stupid planet is even
crappier than it has to be. I walk slowly around the perimeter of
the chamber. All the tunnels look the same, circular tubes about
three meters in diameter, glowing faintly in a way that tells my
conscious mind that there's a positive temperature gradient at
work, and at the same time lets my subconscious know that they
all probably lead directly to hell. I count six paces from each to
the next.

That doesn't seem right either.

No time to worry about it, though. I pick a tunnel and start
walking.

After a half hour or so, I start to wonder if maybe I should have tried to tell Nasha that I wasn't going to just sit there and freeze to death after all. It would be good if she knew not to let Berto file a loss report until and unless I actually die. The Union is pretty loose about a lot of stuff, morality-wise, but some really bad things happened in the early days of bio-printed bodies and personality downloads, and at this point on most colonies you're better off being a serial killer or a child stealer than a multiple.

I pop open a comm window, but of course I'm getting no signal here at all. Too much bedrock between me and the surface. Probably for the best. I'm pretty sure the only reason Nasha didn't force the issue on a rescue attempt is that I gave her the impression that I was broken anyway. If she knew I was up and walking around with nothing worse than a headache and a sprained wrist, she might swing back and try to come for me, whether I wanted it or not.

I can't have that. Nasha's the only clearly good thing I can point to from the past nine years of my life, and if she went down because of me, I couldn't live with myself.

I couldn't, but I'd have to, wouldn't I? I can't die—not and make it stick, anyway.

In any case, I'm not sure she could find me even if she wanted to at this point. It's like an ant farm down here, with cross-tunnels every dozen meters or so. I've tried to pick the ones that looked more up than down, but I don't think I'm having a lot of success, and I have no idea what direction I'm headed.

On the plus side, though, I'm not shivering anymore. I thought at first that I was going hypothermic, but the infrared glow from the walls has been brightening steadily, and I'm pretty sure now that it's getting warmer the deeper I go. I'm actually starting to sweat a little.

Which is okay for now, I guess—but it's gonna suck if I actually do manage to find my way back to the surface. It was negative ten

C when I broke through the crust covering the mouth of that drop shaft. Temperatures at night have been dipping to negative thirty or more, and the wind never stops. If I do find a way out, it might be a good idea to hang around inside until the sun comes back up.

I'M DAYDREAMING ABOUT Nasha the first time I hear the skittering. It's like a bunch of little rocks tumbling down a granite face, except that it starts and stops, starts and stops. I hurry on, and I don't look back. It's obvious to me by now that these tunnels are not a natural formation. I don't know what kind of burrowing animal digs three-meter-wide tunnels through solid rock, but whatever it is, I'm pretty sure I don't want to meet one.

As I press on, the noises come more often, and closer. I find myself walking faster and faster, until I'm almost running. I've just passed a cross-tunnel when I realize that I can't tell if the noises I'm hearing are coming from behind me or in front of me. I pull up short, and turn half around.

And there it is, almost close enough to touch.

It looks generally like a creeper, which I guess makes sense: segmented body, one pair of legs to a segment, hard, sharp claws for feet. The mandibles are different, though. Creepers have one pair on their front segments. This guy has two: a slightly longer pair held parallel to the ground, and a shorter pair held perpendicular to those. Just like a creeper, it has a short, dextrous pair of feeding legs inside the mandibles, and a round, toothy maw.

There are some other important differences. Creepers are pure white—evolved to blend in with the snow, maybe? It's hard to tell from the infrared I'm getting, but I'm guessing that in the visible spectrum this thing would be brown or black.

Also, of course, creepers are maybe a meter long and weigh a few dozen kilograms, while my new friend here is as wide as I am tall, and stretches back down the tunnel as far as I can see.

Fight or flight? Neither one seems like a good bet here. I raise my hands, show it my open palms, and take a slow step back. That gets a reaction. It rears up and spreads both sets of mandibles wide. The feeding legs beckon to me. Body language. To a thing like this, my arms up and spread probably look like a threat. I drop them to my side and take another step back. It slides toward me, its front segments weaving slowly back and forth like the head of a cobra, and I'm thinking I should have listened to Nasha, should have popped my seals and let the local atmosphere do its work, thinking that being eaten by a giant centipede is really not the way I wanted to check out, when it strikes.

The mandibles snap around me, faster than I can react—between my legs, over my right shoulder, and around my waist. The creeper lifts me off the ground, and the feeding legs pin me in place. The maw is opening and closing rhythmically, less than a meter away. There are rows and rows of cold black teeth in there, one behind the other, as far down the furnace-hot gullet as I can see.

It doesn't pull me in, though. It picks me up, and it moves.

The feeding legs are multi-jointed, and they end in nests of tentacles that could almost be fingers, tipped by two-centimeter-long claws. I struggle at first, but they hold my arms splayed and pressed back against the mandibles with a grip like a steel vise. I can kick my feet a little, but I can't reach anything worth kicking. I'm assuming at this point that I'm on my way back to the nest. A snack for the little ones, maybe? Or a special treat for the wife? Either way, if I could reach up to pop my seals now, I'd do it. Not an option, though, so I hang there, imagining what it's going to feel like being ground up in that churning maw.

The trip is a long one, and at one point I actually find myself dozing off. The clacking of the giant creeper's teeth wakes me, though, and I spend the rest of the ride watching them grind against one another as the maw irises open and closed. It's strangely fascinating. The teeth must either grow continuously or fall out and regenerate on a pretty regular basis, because they're really doing a number on each other.

After a while, I realize that the angles at which they strike one another are optimized to keep them sharpened.

We finally stop in a chamber similar to the one I first fell into. The creeper crosses the open space, then slides its head into a smaller side tunnel. I crane my neck around. The passage looks like it dead-ends after twenty meters or so. The family larder, maybe? It sets my feet on the ground, then opens its mandibles. The feeding legs give me a gentle shove, and the head withdraws.

I'm not sure what's happening now, but I'm pretty sure I want to be where that thing is not. I start up the tunnel. There's something strange about the wall at the end. It takes me a few seconds to realize that my ocular is registering visible-range photons for the first time in hours.

When I get to the end of the tunnel, the wall isn't rock. It's hard-packed snow. I put my hand against it and shove. A section a half meter across gives way. Daylight floods in.

At that moment, I suddenly remember being nine years old in my grandmother's country house back on Midgard. It was a sunny spring morning, and I'd caught a spider in my bedroom. I scooped him up in my cupped hands and trapped him, ran down the stairs and out the front door with his sharp little feet scrambling around and around my palms. I crouched down in the front garden, put my hands near the ground, and opened my fingers. As he scuttled away, I felt like a benevolent god.

Through the hole in the wall, I can see the snow-dusted bulge of our main dome, no more than a couple of kilometers away.

I'm the spider. I'm the spider, and that thing in the tunnel just set me down in the garden.

I TRY PINGING Berto, then Nasha, as soon as I'm clear of the tunnel. No response. Not too surprising, I guess. It's early yet, and they were both out on overnights. Would Berto have reported me as KIA as soon as he got back to the dome, or would he have waited until morning? And how long would it take them to actually re-instantiate me after that? I've never been around for that part, so I'm not exactly sure, but I'm guessing it's not very long. I think about leaving a message for Berto, but something tells me to hold off. If he went straight to his rack last night when he got in, I can tell him in person. If not . . . I honestly don't know what happens then, but I've got a weird feeling that I might want to keep my current not-dead status to myself for a while.

It's an hour-long slog through a knee-deep layer of fresh snow back to the perimeter. Despite that, it's actually a nice morning, for a change. The temperature is a hair over zero, for the first time in almost a week. The wind has died down, the sky is a soft, cloudless pink, and the sun is a fat red ball resting just above the southern horizon. We've got a security perimeter established about a hundred meters out from the dome—sensor towers, automated burner turrets, man traps, the works. I've never been sure what the point of this is supposed to be, since the creepers are the only big animals we've seen so far, and they seem to be able to move around under the snow where our sensors can't find them, but it's standard operating procedure, I guess.

Gabe Torricelli is manning the checkpoint leading to the main lock this morning. He's a Security goon, but as goons go he's an okay guy. He's wearing a full kit of powered combat armor, minus the helmet. He looks like an overgrown bodybuilder with a really tiny head.

"Mickey," he says. "You're out early."

I shrug. "You know. Just out for my constitutional. What's with the gear? Did we declare war on somebody while I was on crevasse duty?"

He grins behind his rebreather. "Not yet. Armor's voluntary for picket duty. I just like the way it looks." He gestures back toward the way I came. "Marshall's still got you scouting the foothills, huh?"

"Yup. No point in risking valuable equipment doing scut work when you've got me around, right?"

"Right you are. See anything good out there?"

Yeah, Gabe. I saw a creeper the size of a heavy lift shuttle. It carried me back to the dome and then let me go. Pretty sure it was sentient. Cool, right?

"Nope," I say. "Just a lot of rocks and snow."

"Yeah," he says. "Typical. Marshall's just wasting our time with this bullshit, am I right?"

Ugh. He's bored, and looking to chat. I need to short-circuit this.

"Look," I say. "I'd love to hang, but I've got a thing in the dome this morning. Okay if I head on in?"

"Yeah," he says. "Sure. I guess I don't need to ask for ID, huh?"

"No," I say. "Probably not."

He pulls out a tablet, punches something in, then passes me through and into the dome with a wave. That's good. It might mean nobody's registered Mickey8 with Security yet. Berto's laziness may have saved me an unknowable amount of trouble. On the other hand, it was basically Berto's laziness that got me into this situation in the first place. It would have been difficult, but I'm pretty sure he could have pulled some gear together and come back and extracted me last night.

I wouldn't let Nasha risk coming for me, but Berto? If he'd been willing, I think I would have rolled the dice.

Of course, the whole point of having Expendables is that you don't have to go back for them. Still, no matter how this winds up, I'm going to need to reassess my criteria for picking best friends.

First stop is my rack. I need to get changed, clean up a bit, and put a pressure wrap on my wrist. I don't think it's broken at this point, but it's swollen and purple and I'm guessing it's probably going to be unpleasant for the next few weeks at least. After that, I can get in touch with Berto and make sure he's not getting ready to do something stupid. I need to ping Nasha too, just to let her know I made it out.

Also to say thanks for being willing to try, I guess.

I follow the main corridor two-thirds of the way across the dome, then climb four floors of bare metal spiral staircase to the slums. The low-status racks are up here, dozens of three-by-two-meter rooms separated by extruded plastic dividers and thin foam doors, right up near the roof. My room is near the hub. I've got a double to myself, with enough vertical space to stand up and raise my hands over my head—one of the benefits of being an Expendable, I guess. It's kind of like the way the Aztecs were really nice to their ass-ball players, right up until they dragged them up to the altar and ripped their hearts out.

I first realize we may have an issue when I try to key my door. It's already unlocked. I push it open, heart pounding out a staccato rhythm in my chest. There's someone in my bed, with my blanket pulled up to his chin. His hair is plastered to his forehead, and his face is streaked with what looks like dried snot. I take two steps forward, and swing the door closed behind me. His eyes pop open at the sound of the latch closing.

"Hey," I say.

He sits half up and puts a hand to his face. "What the . . ." He looks at me, and his eyes go wide.

"Crap," he says. "I'm Mickey8, aren't I?"

AT THIS POINT, you may be wondering what I did to get myself designated as an Expendable. Must have been something awful, right? Murdered a puppy, maybe? Pushed an old lady down a staircase?

Nope, and nope. Believe it or not, I volunteered.

The way they sell you on becoming an Expendable is that they don't call it becoming an Expendable. They call it becoming an Immortal. That's got a much nicer ring to it, doesn't it?

I don't want to make it seem like I'm an idiot. I knew what I was getting into, more or less, when I put my thumb to the contract. I sat in the recruiter's office back on Midgard and listened to her entire spiel. Her name was Gwen Johansen. She was a tall, heavyset blonde, with an expressionless face and a voice that sounded like she'd spent most of the morning swallowing gravel. She sat behind her desk, staring down at a screen in her hands, and read off a list of things that I might be required to do that would likely result in the death of that particular instantiation of me.

External repairs during interstellar transit was on the list. So were exposure to local flora and fauna, necessary medical experiments, combat against any hostiles we might encounter, and on and on for so long that I finally tuned out. The plain fact was that it didn't matter what they were going to do to me. I didn't have a choice if I wanted a berth. I wasn't a pilot. I wasn't a medico. I wasn't a geneticist or botanist or xenobiologist. I wasn't even a spear-carrier. I had no practical skills of any sort—but I really, really needed to get the hell off of Midgard, and I needed to do it quickly. This was the first colony ship we'd chartered since our own landfall two hundred years prior, and signing on as an Expendable was the only way I was going to win passage.

I knew that once I submitted my tissue samples and let them run my upload, I'd be first in line for pretty much every dangerous-to-suicidal job that came down the pike. What I didn't really grasp even after hearing Gwen run through the entire litany, though, was how many dangerous-to-suicidal jobs there actually are on a beachhead colony, and how often I'd be called on to perform them. I mean, you'd think that we'd use remotes to handle most of the seriously stupid stuff—stuff like exploring possibly unstable crevasses filled with possibly carnivorous local fauna, just to pick a random example. That's what they did on Midgard, which is why I thought this posting might actually wind up being pretty soft.

Turns out, though, that there's a whole range of things, mostly involving lethal doses of radiation but extending to other abuses as well, that a human body can actually tolerate for a significantly longer period than a mech, and there's a whole other range of things, mostly involving medical experiments and the like, that a mech can't do at all. Moreover, an Expendable is actually a lot easier to replace on a beachhead than a mech is. We won't have any kind of serious mineral extraction, let alone heavy industry, for a long time to come. Any metal lost is lost for good until we can get that stuff up and running. The raw materials they need to make another one of me, on the other hand, just require us to get our agricultural base online.

Not that we've accomplished that either. Getting anything to grow outside the dome on Niflheim is going to be a serious challenge long-term, and something in the local microbiota seems to be screwing with the things we're trying to grow inside as well—but theoretically it's a much more short-term project.

When Gwen was done listing off all of the awful things that might happen to me—several of which actually *have* happened to me, of course—she leaned back in her chair, folded her arms across her chest, and stared at me for a long, awkward moment.

"So," she said finally. "Does this really sound like the sort of job you'd enjoy?"

I gave her what I hoped was a confident smile and said, "Yes, I think it does."

She kept staring, until I could feel little beads of flop sweat forming on my forehead. Have I mentioned that I really, really needed this gig? I was about to say something about how I'd always been comfortable with risk-taking, how I was confident in my ability to stay alive in the most challenging circumstances, when she leaned forward and said, "Are you a total, irretrievable moron?"

That set me back for a moment. "No," I said. "I don't think so, anyway."

"You heard what I said before, right? The whole list?"

I nodded.

"So when I said 'acute radiation poisoning,' for example, you got that. You understood that what I meant by that was that you might well be called upon to perform duties that would result in you deliberately being exposed to a lethal dose of ionizing radiation. You understood that subsequent to that, you would develop a fever, skin rashes, blistering, and eventually that your internal organs would more or less liquefy and leak out of your anus over a period of days, resulting in what I am led to believe is an exceedingly painful death. All of that was entirely clear to you?"

"Yeah," I said, "but that wouldn't really happen, right?"

"Yes," she said. "It very well might."

I shook my head. "Sure, I might get irradiated or whatever, but I wouldn't have some long, drawn-out, agonizing death. I'd just kill myself, right? Take a pill, close my eyes, and wake up as a new me? I mean, that's kind of the point of the whole backup thing, right?"

"Yes," Gwen said. "You'd think that, wouldn't you? The fact is, though, that most Expendables don't."

I waited for her to go on. When it was clear she wasn't going to, I said, "Don't what?"

She sighed. "Kill themselves. My understanding is that that very rarely happens, despite the fact that it would make eminent sense. Apparently three hours of training lectures aren't enough to overcome a billion years of ingrained instinct for self-preservation. Go figure. Also, in many cases the Expendable may be required to ride it out all the way to the bitter end, whether he wants to do so or not. Think about medical experiments, for example. Can't short-circuit one of those with a premature euthanasia. Same with exposure to local microbiota. Command needs to know exactly what biological effects are produced, and they won't let you check out until they've finished gathering data. Understand?"

I nodded. I couldn't think of a more elaborate response. Gwen looked up at the ceiling for a long while. When she finally looked back down at me, I got the feeling that she was disappointed to see me still sitting there.

"So tell me, Mr. Barnes. What, exactly, do you find appealing about the position on offer?"

She set her elbows on the desk then, and rested her chin on her hands.

"Well," I said, "I mean, even if I got killed once or twice, I'd basically be immortal, right? That's what you said."

She sighed again, louder this time. "Right. You're a moron. Ordinarily we try not to discriminate, but the problem in this case is that the Mission Expendable is actually an extremely important posting for a colony expedition. Even a mind as simple as yours obviously is takes up an almost inconceivable amount of storage space. Prepping you for backup is an enormous investment of resources. If you take this position, yours will be the only downloadable personality and the only biological pattern that your colony will carry. That means that if things go badly, you may find yourself the last living thing aboard the *Drakkar,* solely responsible for the welfare of thousands of stored human embryos, among other assets. Is that really a burden you're willing to accept?"

I gave her a nervous smile. She stared me down for what felt like a long time, then leaned back in her chair until the front legs lifted off the floor, folded her hands behind her head, and returned her attention to the ceiling.

"Do you know how many people we've had apply for this particular position?" she asked finally.

"Uh," I said. "No?"

"Guess," she said. "We've had over ten thousand applications for berths on this expedition, all told. Six hundred atmospheric pilots alone have made inquiries. Do you know how many berths we have for atmospheric pilots?"

I know the answer to that question now, because Berto has

mentioned it about a thousand times since we boosted out of orbit, but I didn't have a clue at the time.

"Two," she said. "We've had six hundred pilots apply for two goddamned slots—and these are not weekend-pilot randos. Every single one of those six hundred would be eminently qualified for the job. Miko Berrigan applied to head up our Physics Section. Can you believe that?"

I shook my head. I had no idea who Miko Berrigan was, but apparently he was hell on wheels, physics-wise.

I've since learned that that's true.

I've also since learned that Miko Berrigan is kind of an asshole, but that's not really relevant to the story.

"The point is," Gwen said, "we have had our pick of the litter for this expedition. As I'm sure you're aware, it is a tremendous honor to be selected for a beachhead colony mission, one that most people never even get the opportunity to try for. If we wanted to, we could fill every berth on the *Drakkar* with someone with one green eye and one blue one, and still have a fully qualified crew."

She brought her chair back down onto the floor with a bang then, and leaned across the desk toward me. I had to force myself not to flinch.

"Which brings me back to our Expendable," she said. "Do you know how many applications we've had for that slot?"

I shook my head.

"You," she said. "You are the only person who has stepped forward to fill this particular berth. We were seriously considering asking the Assembly for authority to *conscript* someone until you walked through my door. Now, I can see from your standardized test scores that you are not actually a completely stupid person. In fact, it says here that you're a . . . historian?"

I nodded.

"Is that a job?"

"Actually," I said, "it is—or at least it used to be. The study of history can—"

"Isn't every scrap of known history available to anyone at any time?"

I nodded.

"So what, exactly, makes you more of a historian than me, for example?"

"Well," I said, "I've actually bothered to access a lot of those scraps."

She rolled her eyes. "And someone pays you for this?"

I hesitated. "I suppose it's technically more of a hobby than a job."

She stared me down for five seconds or so, then shook her head and sighed.

"In any case, the post that you are applying for right now is not a hobby. It is most definitely a job, one which, if you take it on, you will never be able to relinquish—and what, exactly, does the fact that nobody else on this entire planet wants this job tell you, Mr. Barnes?"

She looked at me then as if she expected some kind of response, but I honestly had no idea what to say. Finally, she rolled her eyes again, and slid a bio-print reader across the desk to me. I pressed my thumb to the pad, and felt a tiny prick as it nipped off a DNA sample. She took the reader back and glanced down at the display.

"Can I ask a question?" I said.

She looked up at me. Her expression was unreadable. "Sure. Why not?"

"If nobody has applied for this job, if you were actually thinking about *drafting* someone for it, why are you trying so hard to discourage me from taking it?"

She looked back down at her tablet. "An excellent question, Mr. Barnes. I guess maybe you just strike me as a decent sort, and I'd rather this particular job went to an asshole."

She stood then, set the tablet down on her desk, and offered me her hand.

"Whatever," she said. "I guess it's going to you. Welcome aboard."

HERE'S THE QUESTION that Gwen should have asked me, but didn't: What's so rotten about Midgard that you're willing to take a chance on getting your insides liquefied to get away from it? I mean, Midgard's a nice enough place, as third-gen colony worlds go. It sits dead-center in the Goldilocks zone of a red giant that just finished eating its inner system. That means they had to do a bit of terraforming when the first boat showed up, which was probably a pain in the ass. On the plus side, though, unlike our current home, Midgard hasn't been habitable for long enough to have any sophisticated locals to deal with. I'm sure some bad things happened to their Expendable too, but at least he wasn't getting eaten right and left.

Midgard has almost no axial tilt, so there's not much in the way of seasons to worry about. It's warm at the equator and cold at the poles, with a couple of broad, shallow, low-salinity oceans, and one world-girdling continent that completely divides them. Crowding isn't a problem. There were more people in one megacity on old Earth pre-Diaspora than there are on all of Midgard. The beaches are nice. The cities are clean. The government is elected, and mostly limits itself to managing the economy. I never even had a problem with that fat red sun filling half the sky, although I'll admit that the little yellow one we have here already feels more natural somehow.

So, what was the problem? You've probably got a few guesses, so let me run down the list. Love affair gone bad? Nope. I'd had a few girlfriends, some good and some bad, but none bad enough to drive me off-planet, and none at all in the year leading up to my first upload. Money problems? You wouldn't think so, would you? Almost nobody on Midgard had money problems. Virtually the entire industrial and agricultural base was automated, and the government distributed the spinoff on a per-citizen basis, just like nearly every other planet in the Union. In most ways you could measure, Midgard was almost a paradise.

As it turned out, the problem that I had with Midgard was exactly the problem that I had with getting off of Midgard. I wasn't a scientist. I wasn't an engineer. I had no talent for art, or entertainment, or rhetoric. I was—I am—the sort of person who in an earlier age would have been a low-level academic of some sort. I would have read obscure books that I found in obscure archives, and written obscure papers that nobody would ever have read. In an earlier age than that, I might have put in my time in a factory, or a mine, or maybe the infantry. On Midgard, though, there weren't any low-level academics. As Gwen so kindly pointed out, history was anyone's for the taking. With a blink of your ocular, or a few clicks on your tablet, you could know anything you ever needed to know about anything—not that anyone ever bothered to actually do that, of course.

There also weren't any factory jobs, or mining jobs, or even any infantry, for that matter. My standard stipend gave me enough to keep a roof over my head and food in my belly, but try as I might, I couldn't figure out what it was all for. I couldn't think of a single way the universe would be different if I stepped off of my balcony one morning.

And so, like bored young men throughout history, I spent an unfortunate amount of my time finding ways to get myself into trouble.

"So," I say. "It seems like we've got a problem."

I'm in my desk chair, turned to face the bed. Eight is sitting up now, leaning forward with his head in his hands. I know how he feels. Waking up straight out of the tank is like the world's worst hangover, with little bits of leprosy and the bends mixed in for flavor.

"You think? We're screwed, Seven. We're worse than screwed. How did you let this happen?"

I sigh, lean back, and rub my face with both hands. "Which part? The part where Berto assumed I was dead because he was too afraid of getting eaten to come back and rescue me? Or the part where I inconveniently didn't actually die?"

"I don't know. Either one. Could you hand me a towel?"

There's a hand towel hanging over the wardrobe door. I pull it down and toss it to him. He scrubs the worst of the gunk off of his face and neck, then tries to work it back through his hair.

"That's hopeless," I say.

He glares at me and keeps rubbing. "I know that, asshole. I remember when you woke up from the tank, right? I remember when Six woke up, and Five and Three and . . . well, I guess that's all, actually. Anyway, I remember everything you remember."

"Not everything," I say. "I haven't uploaded in over a month."

"Great. Thanks for that."

I sigh. "Don't worry. You're not missing anything good."

He flings the goo-covered towel at me, climbs out of bed, and pulls open the wardrobe. "Haven't been keeping up with the laundry either, huh?"

"Not really. It's been a rough few weeks."

He pulls a grimy sweater and a pair of wind pants down from the top shelf. "Got any clean underwear at all?"

"Check under the bed."

He shoots me a look exactly halfway between hatred and disgust. "What's wrong with you? I don't remember us being a pig."

"I told you. It's been a rough few weeks."

He drops to one knee and pulls a pair of boxers out from under the bed, holds them up at arm's length, then brings them in close and gives them a tentative sniff.

"They're clean," I say. "They just got kicked under there."

He glares at me again, then turns around and dresses himself.

"Thanks," I say. "It's weirdly uncomfortable to look at yourself walking around naked."

"Yeah," he says. "I'm sure it is."

He sits down on the bed again, and runs his hands back through his hair. It's still stiff and shiny black, but at least it's starting to break up into individual strands. It won't look right until he's been through the scrubber a couple of times, though.

"So," he says. "What now?"

I stare at him. He quits playing with his hair and stares back.

"What?" he says.

"Well," I say. "I mean, you shouldn't have come out of the

tank, right? I'm not actually dead. If Command finds out we're a multiple . . ."

His eyes are hard now, and angry. "Say what you mean, Seven."

"Come on," I say. "You know this as well as I do. One of us has got to go."

THE CLOSEST ANALOGUE in the long human story to the Diaspora and the formation of the Union is probably the colonization of Micronesia. The islands of the Pacific back on Earth are small, they're separated by hundreds or sometimes thousands of miles of open ocean, and they were settled by people paddling twelve-meter-long outrigger canoes. When those folks landed on a new island, they had whatever was left in their boats after the journey to tide them over until they could make the new land yield them up something to eat.

That's basically the situation we're in, except that our boats are a little bigger, our journeys are a hell of a lot longer, and we can't even be sure that any of the crops we've brought with us will grow where we make landfall. As a consequence, there is one hard and fast rule that everyone who boards an ark knows and accepts: there are no fat guys in beachhead colonies.

Rations when we made landfall were set at fourteen hundred kilocalories per day, base, with bonuses based on current lean body mass and work schedule. They've been cut back twice since then because, for reasons unexplained, even the hydroponics tanks are having a hard time getting anything to grow here. We're not quite down to cannibalism yet, but most of us are definitely on the gaunt side these days.

The upshot of this is that even if having multiple copies of yourself hanging around at one time weren't the strongest taboo in the Union, there's not a lot of leftovers at dinnertime for a surplus Expendable.

"LOOK," EIGHT SAYS. "If you think I'm just itching to hop into the bio-cycler for you, you're about to be seriously disappointed. I get that this situation isn't one hundred percent your fault, but it's *zero* percent my fault."

I'm pacing back and forth now, which is not very satisfying in a four-by-three room. Eight is sitting on the edge of the bed, elbows on knees, trying to massage the tank-funk out of his temples.

"This isn't about fixing the blame," I say. "It's about fixing the problem."

"Okay, so let's fix both. *You* go jump in the cycler."

I shake my head. "No, that's not gonna happen."

He glares up at me, then grimaces and digs a chunk of hardened tank fluid out of one ear.

"How is this fair? I've been alive for, what, maybe twenty minutes? You've gotten a couple of months, at least. You should be the one to go."

I smile, but not in a friendly way. "Oh no," I say. "Don't try to pull that shit on me. You're thirty-nine years old, just like me. You've got every second of memory and experience that I have, less the six weeks since my last backup. You wouldn't even have known you just came out of the tank if you weren't covered in dried goo."

He stares at me.

I stare at him.

"There's no point in trying to argue this out, Seven. I mean, we can't really compromise on this, can we?" he says finally.

And he's right, of course. This isn't the kind of disagreement where one person or the other just gives up after a while. It's not like picking up the check in a restaurant. We can't take turns.

"Okay," I say. "So what do we do? Take it to Command?"

"No," Eight says, a little too quickly. "Bad idea. Marshall thinks we're an abomination already. If he finds out we're a multiple, he'll kill us both on the spot. We need to keep this between the two of us."

The truth is that if we went to him now, Marshall would probably just say that Eight never should have come out of the tank, and that therefore he should be converted back into slurry without delay. I think about mentioning that now, but . . .

I don't know. Maybe Eight has a point. It does seem unfair somehow to shove him back into the void before he's even had a chance to get the tank goo out of his ears.

What's the alternative, though? I don't want to go down the corpse hole any more than he does.

"Look," I say. "We can figure this out. Let me change my clothes and clean up a bit here. You go hit the chem shower on three, get the rest of the tank gunk off of you, and meet me at the cycler in thirty."

He gives me a wary look, then gets to his feet. "Fine," he says. "Thirty minutes. I'll see you there."

He takes two steps to the door, turns the latch, and pulls it open. He starts out into the corridor, then hesitates and looks back at me.

"Hey. You're not planning on being a dick about this, are you? I mean, you're not gonna call Command while I'm in the shower and try to make this judicial, are you?"

"No," I say. "I won't do that, even though I'm pretty sure I'd win if I did. We'll settle this ourselves."

He smiles. "Thanks, Seven. I'll see you in thirty."

The door swings closed behind him.

I FIGURE EIGHT probably actually needs at least an hour. Tank goo is a nightmare to get off of you, and the chem shower isn't the ideal way to do it. I'm just settling in for a quick nap when there's a soft knock-knock-knock at my door.

"Come," I say. The door swings open. Berto pokes his head in and looks around, then steps through and closes the door behind him.

"Hey, buddy," he says. "How're you feeling?"

Berto takes a seat at my desk, just like I did when I walked in on Eight. Unlike me, though, he doesn't really fit into the chair. Berto's almost two meters tall—a rarity on a beachhead, where compactness is important both for comfort and efficiency. I barely crack one-point-six myself, and I'm pretty average around here. Between the caloric restriction and the fact that he has to slouch and scrunch most of the time, Berto looks an awful lot like a pasty-pale, redheaded stick bug.

I sit up in bed and push my hair back with one hand. I keep my sprained wrist under the blanket. "I'm okay, I guess."

"You look pretty good for being fresh out of the tank," he says. "Been through the scrubber already?"

I nod. He stares at me for a moment, then looks away.

"So," I say. "What happened this time? What happened to Seven?"

Berto shakes his head. "Brother, you do not want to know."

"Huh. Isn't that exactly what you said about Six?"

He looks back at me. "Maybe. I don't know. Does it matter?"

"Yeah," I say. "It kind of does. You're a pilot, right? What's your last, most important duty if you go down?"

His eyes narrow. "Always let them know what killed you."

"Right. It's the same way with Expendables. That's why every time Marshall murders me, he makes me upload right before I check out. I'd like to know what happened to Seven, so I can make sure it doesn't happen to me. And while we're at it, you might as well fill me in on Six too. Whatever got him, I'm sure my constitution can handle it."

Berto stares me down, then shrugs and looks away again. I make a mental note to invite him to play poker for rations sometime. He's a terrible liar.

"Six and Seven both went down the same way," he says. "Swarmed by creepers."

"Okay. Where did this happen, and what was I doing at the time?"

He sighs. "You were out doing one of Marshall's stupid-ass walk-arounds. Over the past few months, he's had you spending most of your time mapping out the crevasses around the dome and scouting them for creepers. Personally I don't really get it, but he seems to have developed some kind of obsession with them." He hesitates, then continues. "Sometimes it seems like you have too, actually. When he first started in on this shit, you complained all the time. A week or so after Seven came out of the tank, though, that stopped. The last few weeks, you just saluted and went. Any idea what that was about?"

I shake my head. "My memories are six weeks out of date. Apparently Seven wasn't keeping up on his uploads."

"Yeah," Berto says. "He mentioned something about that last night when he realized he was going down."

I scratch my chin with my good hand. "Huh. Really? In the middle of getting torn apart by a swarm of creepers, the thing he had on his mind was that he hadn't been uploading?"

Berto's mouth opens and closes twice without making a sound, like a fish pulled out of water. I have to grit my teeth to keep from laughing. He really is a terrible, terrible liar.

"It was before that," he finally manages. "I guess he had a premonition?"

"A premonition."

"Yeah. I mean, I guess so."

I could push on this, but I've got my own secret to keep here, so I decide to let it go.

"Anyway," Berto says, "I dropped Seven off near a crevasse about eight klicks out from the perimeter yesterday afternoon. He had a burner with him. Per usual, he was supposed to be mapping the area and scouting for creepers, with the goal of bringing one back if possible. I was supposed to pick him up on my next circuit."

"But it didn't work out."

"No, it didn't work out. They came up out of the snow all at once, almost as soon as I dropped him, twenty or thirty of them. I was hovering right over him, but they tore him up before I could get the grapple deployed."

I get that he doesn't want to admit that he left me to die down there. That's the kind of thing that could definitely crimp a friend-ship. I'm wondering now, though, about what really happened to Six. Did Berto lie to me about that too?

"Anyway," he says, "I just wanted to come by and make sure you were all set. I thought we could file a quick report with Com-mand, and maybe go grab some breakfast."

I definitely do *not* want to file a report with Command. Not until I settle things with Eight, anyway.

"You know," I say. "I'm actually still pretty whipped. You go ahead and get something to eat. I'm gonna take a quick nap. I'll register with Security when I wake up, and we can file with Com-mand after that."

He gives me a searching look. He knows something's not right here. I usually head straight to the cafeteria after I come out of the tank. Nobody voluntarily skips meals around here, but be-yond that, the bio-printer doesn't print any food into your digestive system. When you wake up, your stomach is pretty much where it would be after a seventy-two-hour fast.

"Okay," he says. "But don't take too long. You know synthesizing your ass takes a huge bite out of our protein budget. Command will want to know what happened, and why, and how we're planning on making up the deficit. This is your second regen in the last eight weeks, so we'll need to come up with something good this time."

"We could just tell them what actually happened."

He shakes his head. "We have to be a little creative with this. Command is really sensitive about losing calories and protein from the system right now, and Marshall is not about to accept responsibility for it, even though these stupid sorties are on his orders. He's probably going to be pissed at you for not defending yourself adequately, and he's definitely going to be pissed at me for not swooping in and recovering your body. Honestly, if this keeps up, he may just refuse to authorize your regen one of these times."

A shiver runs up my spine. Was that a premonition?

"Hey," he says. "Are you okay? You don't look so good, Mickey."

I rub my eyes with my right hand, and hope he doesn't notice that my left hasn't come out from under the blanket this entire time.

"Yeah," I say. "I'm good. Just need to sleep off the tank funk. I'll meet you at the caf in an hour."

He looks me up and down, then gets to his feet, reaches over, and pats me on the leg.

"Good man. I'll save you some cycler paste."

"Thanks, Berto. You're a pal."

"By the way," he says, just as the door is closing behind him.

"I couldn't help but notice that you've had your hand on your junk the entire time I've been here. Careful with that. Nasha gets jealous."

"Yeah, Berto. I know. Thanks for noticing, though."

"No problem. See you in an hour."

I can hear him snickering as the latch clicks closed.

I'VE DIED SIX times in the past eight years. You'd think I'd be used to it by now, wouldn't you?

To be fair, one of those was a surprise, one was an emergency situation, and one of my instantiations refused to upload before he died. I only remember what gets uploaded, so all I know about what happened to those iterations of me is what Nasha or Berto told me, or what I've seen on surveillance vids. The other three, though, were planned, and standard procedure is to have the Expendable upload as close to his termination as possible, basically for the reason I gave Berto—the next iteration needs to know what happened to the last one, so that hopefully he can keep it from happening again. So, I guess I'm more familiar with the hollow feeling that's settling into the pit of my stomach right now than most people ever get to be.

This isn't exactly like any of those times, of course. For one thing, those other Mickeys knew for shit sure they were going to die. Unless Eight is planning to shiv me or something, I've only got a fifty-fifty chance of going down this time.

I'm not really sure that's a good thing. There's a certain peace that comes from knowing without a doubt what's going to happen to you. The possibility that I might survive this morning is a source of anxiety as much as it is a source of hope.

The uncertainty isn't the big difference between this time and those others, though. The big difference is that up until now, every time I went down I could at least halfway believe the crap my handlers were feeding me about my own immortality. I knew that a few hours after Mickey3 died, Mickey4 would come out of the tank, and I could imagine that it would just be me both times, closing my eyes and then opening them.

If I die now, though, there won't be another me coming out of the tank. The other me is already here, and despite all appearances, Eight is most definitely not a continuation of me.

Honestly, he doesn't even seem to like me very much.

THE CYCLER IS on the lowest level, and halfway across the dome from my rack. It's not a long walk, realistically speaking, but it feels like one this morning. The corridors are nearly empty, and as I pace down them the only sounds are my footfalls and the pounding rush of blood in my ears. I know it's irrational, but deep in my belly I can feel that this isn't going to go my way. When I take the two shallow steps up to the entrance to the cycler chamber, it's like I'm mounting the stairs to the gallows.

The bio-cycler is the heart and soul of any beachhead colony. It takes our shit, our tomato stems, our potato peels and rabbit bones and half-chewed gristle, our hair clippings and fingernails, our dropped-off scabs and wadded-up tissues, and eventually our corpses. In return, it gives us protein paste and vitamin slurry and fertilizer. Nobody wants to live on cycler paste, but a desperate colony can do it for a very long time.

The cycler works by breaking down anything you drop down the corpse hole into its component atoms, then piecing them back together in whatever order you specify. This takes an obscene amount of energy, but our power plant is an antimatter-driven starship engine. Energy is the one thing we have more than enough of.

I've finished transmitting my access code to the control console when Eight walks in. I lift the safety cover and press the big red button, and the corpse hole irises open in the center of the floor.

The corpse hole is one of those things we try not to think too much about. I've only seen it open on the rare occasions that I've been seconded out to garbage duty, and I've never really looked inside. I'm not sure what you'd expect an antimatter-driven, all-devouring maw to look like—roaring flames and a stench of sulfur, maybe?—but it's actually quiet and odorless and kind of pretty. It's just a flat black disk at first, but then the disassembler field starts grabbing dust motes, and they disappear one by one in tiny firefly flashes.

It doesn't look so bad.

Better than being ripped apart by a swarm of creepers, anyway.

"So," Eight says. "You ready?"

I shrug. "Yeah, I guess so. Kinda regretting not going judicial at this point, to be honest, but let's do this."

He smiles, and claps me on the shoulder. "You're okay, Seven. I'm gonna feel really bad when I shove you down that hole."

My heart stutters. "What do you mean, shove me?"

His smile disappears. "Think about it. Do you really want to go into that thing conscious?"

Huh. That's a good point. Actual corpses get lowered into the hole pretty slowly. I don't know what the maximum feed rate is, but if it's less than infinite, unconscious or already deceased is probably a smarter way to go.

Eight turns to stand next to me, looking down into the hole.

"You know," he says, "you could still do the decent thing, and volunteer to be the one to go."

"Sure," I say. "So could you."

He puts his arm around my shoulder. "Not gonna happen, huh?"

"Probably not."

The disk has gone black again. Out of dust, I guess. Eight hawks up a glob of tank goo and spits. It flashes when it hits the threshold, sizzles for a second, and disappears.

"This may be less painless than I thought," he says.

"Truth," I say. "Tell you what—I could strangle you first, then push you through."

He grins. "Thanks, Seven. You're a real humanitarian."

We stand in silence for a while. His arm around my shoulder grows heavier and heavier. Finally, I step out from under it and turn to face him.

"Look," I say. "Are we doing this?"

"I guess so," he says.

He raises his left hand. I raise my right. We clench our fists and say the words together.

"One . . ."

"Two . . ."

"Three . . ."

"Shoot."

I'm planning to go with Rock, right up until we shoot. But then I remember that he's me. He's probably thinking the same thing. So it's Paper, right? But what if he's thinking that too? He could be figuring I'll go with Paper and shooting Scissors. So that brings me back to Rock, which is good because by the time I work my way through all of that it's too late and my fist is still clenched.

I look down.

His hand is held out flat.

"Sorry, brother," he says.

Yeah, sorry.

Thanks for that, asshole.

KNEELING THERE ON the decking, my face six inches from the disassembler field interface, looking at the prospect of being converted into slurry for the hungry colonists of Niflheim, I find myself once again contemplating the question of whether I made the right call when I pressed my thumb down onto that reader pad back in Gwen Johansen's office nine years ago.

Even now, though, I have to say—yeah, I did. No question about it, really.

I didn't go home after I left Gwen's office. I would've liked to, because I was hungry and tired and could've used a shower. I couldn't, though, for the same reason that I couldn't say no to Gwen's oh-so-tempting offer of half-assed immortality. I'd gotten onto Darius Blank's shit list, you see—and as far as I could tell, I didn't have any reasonable way to get back off of it.

The root of this particular problem, like the root of pretty much all of my problems, now that I think of it, was Berto.

Berto was the only person on the *Drakkar* that I'd known before I gave Gwen my DNA and signed my life away. We met in school, where he was tall, smart, athletic, and weirdly good-looking considering how he turned out, and I was . . . well, I was pretty much what I am now, only smaller. We bonded over our common love of the flight simulator, which he mastered in about an hour and which I was still crashing when we graduated, and our hatred of the school administrators, who hated me right back for obsessing about *history* when I could have been studying something useful, but despite all our best efforts loved Berto like the son they'd never had. In form ten, Berto's calculus instructor told him he should reconsider spending so much time with me if he wanted to reach his full potential.

I think Berto took that as just another challenge.

The thing you have to understand about Berto is that he was one of those obnoxious kids who was prodigy-level good at nearly everything he ever tried. When we were fifteen, his mom bought him a pog-ball racket. He didn't take lessons. He didn't join a recreational league. He spent a couple of months banging balls off of the wall of the admin building after classes to figure out how it worked, did one season on the school team, then turned around and entered a pro-am tournament. Nobody had any idea who he was when he showed up for his first match. He won that one going away, and by the end of the week he'd finished second in his age bracket. The next year, he won the amateur division. The summer after we graduated, he started playing for money. By the time he dropped the game to start serious flight training two years later, he was the tenth-ranked player on the planet.

All of which would have been apropos of nothing, except that nine years after that, I was living in an extremely unfashionable apartment in an extremely unfashionable part of Kiruna, and Berto had been selected for the crew of the *Drakkar*. We were sitting in a café called Shaky Joe's, sipping tea and killing time while we waited for a ball game to start on the viewscreen over the bar, when he mentioned that he was considering coming out of retirement for one last run at the spring pro-am before disappearing into the unknown forever.

"Think about it," he said. "If I take that trophy after all this time, I'll be a legend. They'll still be talking about me a hundred years from now."

I opened my mouth to tell him that he'd be a legend, all right, but it wouldn't be because he'd won a global tournament and then ridden off into the sunset. It would be because he thought he could do that after being out of the game for nine years, and then he'd lost his first match to some eighteen-year-old by a hundred points.

I didn't say that, though. I didn't because it suddenly occurred to me that while *I* knew that for the past nine years he'd been spending nearly every minute that he wasn't in the air or in orbit hanging around with me, most of the people in Kiruna did not. They still remembered twenty-year-old Berto Gomez beating seasoned pros and hardly seeming to break a sweat doing it. They remembered him doing things with a racket that people hadn't realized could be done up until then, and they remembered commentators calling him the most naturally talented player they'd ever seen. They didn't have any idea that he basically hadn't touched a racket in the past nine years.

"Yeah," I said. "Do it, man. You'll be a freaking *legend*."

So, he did. He registered for the tournament, and one of the news feeds picked up the story and did an interview with him that they paired with footage from his last tournament, which he'd won without dropping a single game.

Meanwhile, I scraped up every credit I had, and a bunch that I didn't, and I placed a bet on Berto to lose his first match.

I don't have a great defense for this decision, except to say that the market for amateur historians in Kiruna wasn't great, I had no real prospects for any kind of gainful employment, and the idea of living out the rest of my life on a basic subsidy was so depressing that I couldn't contemplate it.

Was it worse than the prospect of being dissolved headfirst? Maybe not, but I wasn't thinking along those lines yet.

You can probably see where this is going.

By the time Berto won the goddamned tournament, I was so far underwater from doubling down and doubling down again that even if I'd somehow found an actual paying job somewhere, it would have taken me half a lifetime to get back to the surface.

The person I was underwater to, specifically, was Darius Blank.

Vids are full of stories about guys who fall behind on their gambling debts and get murdered for it, but that's not actually how it usually works. After all, while it may be hard to collect a debt from a live guy, it's indisputably even harder to collect from a dead one—and in the end, collecting the debt is all somebody like Darius Blank really cares about. I wasn't worried about him killing me. I guess I had some vague idea that he'd garnish my subsidy, and maybe make me work as his valet or something. It would be unpleasant, but I'd survive.

Berto, to his credit, did his best to convince me that I was mistaken about all of this.

Also to his credit, Berto felt bad about what his win had cost me. He had a suggestion for how he could make it up to me. He wanted me to sign on to the *Drakkar*.

He had some vague idea that he could get me in as a Security goon. He was famous, after all, and he'd always gotten whatever he wanted up until that point in his life. Why wouldn't he be able to get this?

Gwen Johansen pretty much summed up the answer to that question for me during our interview. There were a lot of people who wanted Security berths, and there were only eighteen slots available. Most of them went to people with both some sort of qualification—experience in law enforcement, weapons training, etc.—and political connections. I didn't have any of those things, because having read extensively about the Battle of Midway does not count as military experience, and as it turned out Berto didn't have nearly as much pull as he thought he did.

I did put in a request to interview for a Security position. A rejection bounced back to me less than a second later.

The next afternoon I met Berto for coffee at Shaky Joe's. I showed him the rejection notice on my tablet.

"Ouch," he said. "That sucks."

"Yeah," I said. "It was kind of a dumb idea, anyway. I owe some money. You don't flee the planet over something like that."

Berto shook his head. "You owe a lot of money, Mickey, and guys like Darius Blank don't forgive and forget. What is it, a hundred thousand credits? How are you planning on paying that back?"

I shrugged. "Installment plan?"

"You didn't just buy a used flitter, buddy."

"Yeah," I said. "I know." I dropped my head into my hands. "I'm such an idiot. I can't believe I didn't just tell you to throw the freaking match."

He stared at me for a long moment, then laughed. "You could have asked," he said, "but I wouldn't have done it. This tournament was the last thing the yahoos on this planet will ever hear from me, Mickey. There's no way I wasn't going to win."

That's the thing about Berto. Friendship with him only ever went so far, and no farther.

On the way home from the coffee shop, I remember thinking that this really wasn't going to be so bad. Yeah, Blank would take a chunk of my subsidy, but he'd have to leave me enough to stay alive, right? If I starved to death, he'd never get his money back. And maybe being his valet wouldn't be so bad? It would give me a reason to get out of the apartment, anyway.

I got home. I took the lift tube up to my floor. I let myself into my apartment. The door was still swinging shut behind me when my legs stopped working and I fell flat on my face.

"Hello, Mickey," a voice said. I tried to answer, but my mouth wasn't working either, and all that came out was a low moan. "Just relax," the voice said. "This won't take long." Something pressed against the back of my neck.

I spent the next thirty seconds in hell.

I later learned that the thing that had been pressed against my neck was in fact a neural inducer. It was tuned to tap directly into my pain centers. It didn't do any physical damage, but if you're curious about what I experienced, try skinning yourself alive while a friend works you over with a blowtorch.

That might get you about ten percent of the way there.

When it was over, I was astonished to find that I was still alive. I was sobbing and paralyzed and I'd soiled myself, but I was still alive. A hand patted my shoulder.

"This was fun," the voice said. "We'll be working together, you and I, until you're all square with Mr. Blank. See you tomorrow, Mickey."

He didn't close the door behind himself on the way out.

It was about an hour before I could move again. I got to my feet, staggered into the bathroom, and cleaned myself up. That taken care of, I sat down and had a good cry.

That night, I logged on to the recruitment page for the *Drakkar*. It listed the various sections and positions, and who had been selected for each so far.

Every slot was full.

Every one but one.

I pinged Berto.

"Hey," I said. "What's an *Expendable*?"

"That," Berto said, "is the one berth on the *Drakkar* that you do *not* want."

"It's the only one that's still open. I want it."

He was silent for a while. When he spoke again, his voice had the tone you take when you're explaining to someone that you want them to come down off the ledge.

"Look," he said. "Don't get me wrong about this. I would really love to have you with me on this trip. This is a one-way, and it would be great to have a friend along. But Mickey—"

"Can you put in a word for me?"

"I mean—"

"Berto," I said. "I'm asking for your help here. You kind of did this to me, you know."

"I didn't," he said. "I didn't tell you to bet against me. If you'd asked, I would have told you to bet *on* me. I knew I was going to win."

"Will you help me?"

He sighed. "Honestly, Mickey? I don't think you're gonna need my help."

He cut the connection. I went back to the recruitment page and scheduled an interview for the next afternoon.

Twelve hours later, when Gwen ran down her list of all the horrible things that might happen to me during my tenure as an Expendable, all I could think was, *That doesn't sound so bad, actually*. They put some effort into training me not to fear the reaper once I'd boosted up to the *Drakkar* and couldn't change my mind about signing on, but honestly none of that made too much of an impression on me. I'd gotten all the training anyone ever needed on that front in that one afternoon.

I DON'T GET shoved into the cycler at this time. The disassembler field doesn't get me.

I'm explaining this now because you looked nervous.

I'm on my hands and knees, looking down at the hole. Swear to God, I'm gonna do it. I lower my face down, right next to the interface. I can feel the field pulling at me, a tingle along my cheeks and across the bridge of my nose as it strokes my skin, and I'm trying to figure out a way to do this that will be something less than agonizing, when I feel a hand on my shoulder.

"Give me a minute!" I bark, picturing Eight shoving me down the hole face-first.

"No," Eight says. He pulls me back onto my heels and offers me a hand up. "This isn't right. I can't just stand here and watch you do this."

I let him haul me to my feet. I'm shaking so badly that I can barely stand.

"Okay," I say. "I'm with you on that."

I take a deep breath, then another. For some reason, staring down into that black disk was much, much worse than staring down the gullet of that thing in the tunnel last night.

"So, ah . . . what do you suggest?"

"Let's go back upstairs," he says. "I can drown you in the toilet, then chop you up in the chem shower and feed you through the cycler a piece at a time."

I stare at him. He's grinning.

"Too soon," I say finally. "Much too soon. Seriously, Eight, what are we doing here? We've still only got one berth, and one ration card. More importantly, we've only got one registered identity. If *anybody* finds out we're a multiple . . ."

He shrugs. "These are unusual circumstances, right?"

"Yeah, maybe—but given the resource constraints we're under, I don't think Command is likely to be sympathetic. If we go to Marshall now, one of us is definitely going down that hole."

"Most likely," he says. "And if we try to be sneaky about it, there's a fair chance both of us wind up as slurry."

I squeeze my eyes closed and wait for my pulse to slow from jackhammer to frightened baby bird, then finally to something close to normal. When I open them, Eight is looking at me with concern that's clearly bordering on alarm.

"You okay, Seven?"

"Yeah," I say. I shake my head and breathe in, breathe out. "I'm good. They talk about staring death in the face, but . . ."

"A bit too literal, huh?"

"Right," I say. "If Marshall does wind up feeding me to the cycler, I really, really hope he has the decency to kill me first."

Eight puts one hand to my shoulder. "You and me both, brother. In the meantime, though, we need some kind of plan."

"Agreed. Do you have one?"

He runs both hands back through his hair. "I don't know . . . I don't know . . . they didn't cover this situation in training."

That's the truth, anyway. Training was one hundred percent about dying. I don't remember them dedicating much time at all to staying alive.

"Look," he says. "We've got a heavy ration card. Unless you've done something stupid since our last upload, we should still be getting two thousand kcal a day."

"Yeah," I say. "I think that's right."

"So if we split that down the middle, we've got enough to keep us alive for a while. Not happy, maybe, but alive."

I can feel my face twisting into a grimace. "A thousand kcal a day each? That's brutal, Eight. We have to be able to do better than that. What about Berto? This is mostly his fault. If we told him what's going on, think he might feel guilty enough to kick in a little cycler paste?"

Eight looks doubtful. "Maybe. I'd rather save that for desperation time, though. Berto's not the most altruistic guy on Niflheim, and I don't know how much of a fundamentalist he is about the multiple thing."

"Yeah," I say. "You make some good points. Also, he abandoned me to die in a cavern last night, so you can put that on the maybe-don't-trust-him side of the scales."

"Right," he says. "That. Okay. What about petitioning Marshall for a bump in our ration?"

I roll my eyes. "Sure. I'll get right on that."

"Look," Eight says. "When I stopped by the caf on my way down here, paste was selling at a twenty-five percent discount. If we stick to nothing but, that's twelve hundred and fifty kcal of actual nutrition each. It's not great, but . . ."

"Okay," I say. "Fine. I guess we won't starve to death right away, anyway. That still doesn't address our main problem, though. *There's two of us.* Marshall looks like he just stepped in something rotten every time he has to deal with the fact that there's one Mickey Barnes in his colony. If he gets a sniff of this, the cycler is a best-case scenario for us."

I should point out here that Commander Marshall found out about my run-in with Darius Blank about a week after we boosted out of orbit around Midgard, and interpreted that as evidence that a criminal element had infiltrated his colony. Add that to the fact that he comes from a religious tradition that considers the whole concept of pulling people out of the tank even one at a time to be an abomination, and you wound up with me about thirty seconds from being chucked out of an air lock before the captain of the *Drakkar*, a very nice woman named Mara Singh who is now head of our Engineering Section, reminded him that he wasn't actually in command of the mission until we made landfall on Niflheim.

Somehow, I don't think this situation is likely to improve his opinion of me.

"I know," Eight says. "I know . . . but unless you want to change your mind about going down the hole today, there's nothing we can do about that point, is there?"

"No," I say. "I guess not."

"Of course, if you did change your mind?"

"Don't worry, Eight. You'll be the first to know."

He's grinning. I'm definitely not.

"Thanks," he says. "Hey—what about Nasha? Do you think we can talk to her about this?"

I have to think about that one. Nasha and I have been together since I was Mickey3, and unlike Berto, she was ready to risk her one and only life to pull me out of that hole last night. If there was one person we could trust around here, she'd be it.

On the other hand, if we eventually do wind up in front of Marshall over this, I'd really, really rather she didn't have to go down with us.

"You know what?" I say. "Let's just keep this between us for now, huh?"

"Sure," Eight says. "I mean, the way things have gone since landfall, one of us will be dead pretty soon anyway, right? Problem solved."

Ugh. He's probably right about that.

ON THE TOPIC of being dead soon, here's a story for you: a few months after landfall, when I was still Mickey6, Berto took me out for a ride-along. We took up a fixed-wing, single-engine reconnaissance flitter that day instead of one of the heavy lifters that he usually flies. We were already up and circling over the dome when I asked him how they managed to fit a gravitic generator into such a tiny plane. He turned to look at me, a subtle smile on his face.

"Gravitics? You're kidding, right?"

"No," I said. "I'm not."

He shook his head, then throttled up and put us into a steep, banking climb.

"This is an aircraft, Mickey. The only thing keeping us up here is Bernoulli's principle."

I didn't have any idea who Bernoulli was or what principles he might have had, but I really didn't like the sound of that. I'd never been off the ground before without the sure knowledge that I was surrounded by a gravitic field that would not, under any circumstances, allow me to plunge into the ground at a hundred and fifty meters per second and burst open like an overripe melon.

"Berto?" I said. "Do you think you might want to level out or something? Or better yet, maybe head back in and switch this thing out for something a little more stable?"

He laughed. "Are you serious? Do you have any idea how

much wheedling I had to do to get them to let me sign out the flitter? The whole point of taking this thing out today is that it can do things that a heavy lifter can't."

I opened my mouth to say something about not really wanting to do things that a heavy lifter can't, but before I could get anything out we were in a barrel roll and I was screaming like a . . . well, like one of what I was, I guess, which was someone who was suddenly, shamelessly, gut-churningly terrified of dying.

I think that's when I first realized that despite all the training, despite the indoctrination, despite the incontrovertible fact that I'd died five times by then and I was clearly still alive—deep down, in my heart of hearts, I did not believe in immortality.

"So," Nasha says, "what's with the pauper's breakfast?"

I'm halfway through choking down a six-hundred-kcal bowl of unsweetened cycler paste. I should note here that in the economy of a beachhead colony, a kcal is not actually a kcal. Different items can come at anything from a steep discount to a premium, depending on how closely they resemble something that you'd actually want to put into your mouth. Like Eight said, paste and slurry are trading at a twenty-five percent discount at the moment, which means that if I stick to nothing but, I can probably hold most of my body weight for at least a week or two. Nasha's working on a mashed yam and Cajun-blackened cricket scramble. That's going at par this morning. They actually have a few rabbit haunches and some sickly-looking tomatoes on offer, but those are at a forty percent premium. I'm guessing I can forget about that kind of luxury as long as Eight is still around.

"Well," I say. "I've been thinking about doing some body-building. Thought maybe if I max out my calories and bulk up a little, it'll take the creepers longer to eat me next time."

She giggles. Nasha's giggle is one of her best features. It's soft and delicate, and when she giggles she has a tendency to look to the side and cover her mouth with her hand. The effect is so at odds with her whole badass-combat-pilot thing that it's almost like she becomes a different person.

"I'm glad you've still got a sense of humor about this," she says. "You've been going down pretty often since we made landfall. Some folks might be getting bitter by now."

I refill my water glass. Cycler paste really isn't meant to be eaten by itself. It doesn't taste like anything in particular, but it's thick and gritty enough that it needs a lot of washing down.

"Well," I say, "I try to look at it this way. If Seven hadn't gotten himself whacked, I never would have come out of the tank, right?"

Her face clouds over. "I guess," she says.

I look up from my shitty breakfast. "What?"

She shakes her head. "This is hard for me, Mickey, and every time you go down it gets harder. I felt awful last night—worse than I did when Six died, maybe even worse than I did after what happened to Five. Even after you told me you were shutting down, I hung around just in comm range, hoping you'd change your mind. When I finally gave up and came back to the dome, I spent an hour in the bay sitting in my cockpit and crying like a baby. Now, though, here you are, and like you said, if I *had* saved you last night, *this* you wouldn't be here . . . and now I don't know what to feel."

"Yeah," I say. "Immortality is confusing, huh?"

"Right you are," says Berto. I look around to see him standing behind me, a tray of yams and crickets in his hands.

"Morning, Berto," Nasha says. "Have a seat. I guess."

He sets his tray down next to mine and folds himself onto the bench. "What's up with the gruel, Mickey? And what happened to your hand?"

I look down. I've got my wrist wrapped up tight, but you can still see bits of purple bruising sticking out around the edges.

"I fell getting out of bed," I say. "Tank funk, right?"

Berto gives me a long look, and I can see the wheels turning. "Right," he says. "When, exactly, did this happen?"

"After you stopped by my rack," I say. "Why do you care?"

Nasha looks up from her breakfast. "Am I missing something?"

"Maybe," Berto says. "How long after I stopped by?"

"I don't know. Right before I came down here. Maybe half an hour ago?"

"Your wrist was fine when I saw you in the shower room," Nasha says.

"Right," I say. "It was after that."

Berto's eyes narrow, and he shakes his head.

"Seriously," Nasha says. "What's going on?"

"I'm not sure," Berto says. "Mickey? What's going on?"

I spoon up the last of my cycler paste. I'm wondering if Berto might have run into Eight on his way down here. If so, I need to come clean now and hope he's willing to keep his mouth shut. If not, though . . .

"Nothing's going on," I say. "I'm just trying to finish my breakfast."

I take a quick look around. We're late for breakfast now, but early for lunch. There's nobody sitting close enough to us to overhear what we're saying. Berto's still staring at me.

"So?" I say. "What are you getting at, Berto?"

He takes a forkful of crickets and yam, chews slowly, and swallows. "I dunno, Mickey. I've seen you come out of the tank a lot lately. Something's just a little off about you this time."

I feel my face twist into a scowl. "Maybe if you focused less on how I act when I come out of the tank and more on not getting me killed and back in the tank in the first place, we wouldn't be having this discussion."

"Oh yeah," Nasha says. "There's the bitter."

"Anyway," Berto says, "I didn't sit down here so that I could get into it with Mickey over how he hurt his jerking hand. I was actually wondering if either of you had heard anything about what happened on the perimeter this morning."

Nasha grimaces into the remains of her breakfast and pokes halfheartedly at a scorched potato skin.

"I heard I'm on sweep again in an hour, even though I just came off shift four hours ago. I assumed there was a reason, but nobody's said shit to me about what it is."

Berto leans across the table toward her and drops his voice. "We lost someone."

"Lost?" Nasha says. "Lost how?"

Berto shrugs. "Nobody seems to know. It was the Security goon manning the east checkpoint. Dani said it was Gabe Torricelli. He pinged in at eight, but not at eight thirty. When they sent someone out to look for him, all they found was a bunch of churned-up snow."

I've already opened my mouth to say I saw Gabe this morning before I remember that neither of these two are supposed to know I was outside the dome today. Gabe was the one who waved me in when I got back from the labyrinth. That must have been around . . .

Eight fifteen?

Holy shit.

Did the creepers follow me back to the dome?

I flash back to that spider I set free in the garden all those years ago. What if that's not what happened at all last night? What if I was actually an ant they didn't stomp so that they could figure out where the nest is?

"What?" Nasha says.

I look from her to Berto, then back again. They're both staring at me.

"Seriously," Berto says. "You look like you just wet yourself, Mickey. What the hell? Were you tight with this guy?"

That's kind of a stupid question, considering that there are fewer than two hundred humans on this planet, and we've been cooped up with all of them for the past nine years. It says something about how little the three of us have interacted with our fellow colonists that, no, I was not tight with Gabe. In fact, I barely knew him beyond recognizing his face and having a vague sense that he wasn't one of the bad ones—and neither, obviously, did either of them.

"I know who he was," I say. "We weren't really friends. Does it matter, though? We just lost like point-six percent of our population, Berto."

"Yeah," Berto says. "I guess that's true. I wasn't actually a big fan of old Gabe, to be honest. During transit, he was one of those guys who was constantly busting people's asses about not putting in enough time in the carousel. You make a point, though. Until we start thawing out embryos, we really can't afford too many leaks in the bottom of the gene pool."

"I'm not worried about that," Nasha says. "I mean, if we need more generic white guys around here, we can always just crank out a few more Mickeys, right?"

They both laugh. I hesitate a bit too long before joining in.

"Seriously, though," Berto says. "Mickey does have a point."

I don't actually remember making any points, but okay.

"Truth," Nasha says. "Pretty sure Gabe didn't just wander off."

"Creepers got him," Berto says.

Nasha looks up from the last of her yams. "You know that?"

"Not for sure, but what else could it have been? We haven't seen anything else on this rock yet that's bigger than an amoeba."

Nasha shakes her head. "Creepers coming that close to the dome is bad news. Creepers taking down an armed goon is worse. Was he armored up?"

He was—but again, I'm not supposed to know that.

"Dunno," Berto says. "Probably not, though. No reason to be up until now, right? I mean, this is the first time the creepers have actually killed somebody."

"They killed me," I say. "Twice, actually."

Berto puts one arm around my shoulders and gives me a squeeze. "I know they did, buddy."

Nasha snickers. I shoot her a glare, but she's back in her breakfast and doesn't notice. I expect that kind of shit from Berto. Nasha's usually better than that.

"Armor or no," Berto says, "Gabe would have been carrying a heavy-duty burner, right? How do you get yourself killed by a bunch of bugs when you're armed with something that can flash-fry a buffalo?"

"Burners don't affect them," I say.

They both turn to look at me.

"What?" Nasha says.

"Yeah," Berto says. "What are you talking about, Mickey?"

I open my mouth to answer, then let it fall closed again when I see Berto's eyes widen. Again, I need to get him into a poker game.

"I feel like I'm missing something," Nasha says. "Friends don't keep secrets, Mickey."

"No," Berto says. "No, Mickey's right, actually. He had a burner when he got taken down last night. It didn't do him any good. I guess I forgot about that."

I give him my best dead-eye stare. "You forgot?"

"Yeah," he says. "I forgot."

"You forgot that you saw your best friend get torn to shreds less than twenty-four hours ago."

"Well," Berto says, "I don't know if I'd say *best* friend."

"Torn apart?" Nasha says. "I thought he wound up freezing to death at the bottom of a crevasse."

I give Berto my best confused-yet-angry look. "What's this about freezing to death, Berto?"

He shoots a quick, poisonous glare at Nasha, then shakes his head and says, "Not important. The point is, you went down, and there was nothing any of us could do about it."

"Not true," Nasha says, and goes back to poking at her breakfast. "I could have." She looks up at me, gives me a sad half smile. "He wouldn't let me. You were brave last night, Mickey. You wouldn't let me risk myself for you. Can't take that away from you, no matter how dumb you were to fall down that hole in the first place." Her smile fades then, replaced by a scowl. "Anyway, the actual point here is that, however he managed to do it, Gabe Torricelli got himself killed or kidnapped or eaten this morning, and because of that I now have to pull a double goddamned shift aloft." She looks over at Berto. "Speaking of which—why are you off duty this morning? You didn't spend any more time up last night than I did."

Berto shrugs. "I guess Marshall just likes me more."

That's still hanging in the air between us when a chat window pops up in my ocular.

<Command1>:You are required to report to Commander Marshall's office no later than 10:30. Failure to report will be considered insubordination and will result in a reduced ration allocation. Please acknowledge.

I've just bounced back a read receipt when a second window opens next to the first, partially covering Nasha's face with text.

<Mickey8>:You're seeing the summons from Command too, right?
<Mickey8>:Yeah, I see it.
<Mickey8>:Ugh. We're both Mickey8 now, huh?

<Mickey8>:Looks like it.

<Mickey8>:Great. This is gonna be confusing.

<Mickey8>:I'm sure we'll figure it out.

<Mickey8>:Think the network's gonna flag the fact that the same handle is pinging from two different locations?

<Mickey8>:Probably not unless somebody goes digging.

<Mickey8>:In which case, we're screwed anyway.

<Mickey8>:Right.

<Mickey8>:Anyway, I'm guessing this summons is Marshall looking to chew on us for getting killed again, and wasting seventy kilos of colony protein. You mind handling it? I've got a serious case of tank funk, and I could really use a nap.

<Mickey8>:Do I have a choice?

<Mickey8>:Zzzzzzz

I blink both windows closed. Berto and Nasha are staring at me. "Rude," Nasha says.

"Yeah," Berto says. "Extremely." He pushes back from the table, stands, and picks up his tray. "That said, I've gotta run. Have a fun time out there, Nasha."

Nasha picks up a scrap of yam skin with her fork and flings it at his back as he walks away. I have to resist the urge to chase the scrap down and eat it.

"Anyway," Nasha says when he's gone, "I've got an hour to kill before I have to go up again. Want to finish what we started in the shower?"

It takes me a second or two to put that together with what she said earlier about seeing me in the shower room and realize what she must be talking about, then another two or three to get the image of her with Eight out of my head. I can't actually be jealous of myself, can I?

Yes, apparently I can.

Doesn't matter, though. For better or worse, I've got somewhere to be.

"Actually," I say, "I just got a ping from Command. I've got to go pay Marshall a visit."

"Oh," she says. "Right. Pissed about you flushing another hunk of protein down the toilet, huh?"

"Yeah," I say. "Probably something like that."

She half stands, leans across the table, grabs me by the back of the head, and pulls me into a kiss.

"Don't take any shit from him," she says. "Getting iced is your job, and you were out there on orders. He can't be mad at you for being a klutz." She kisses me again, this time on the forehead. "I'm gonna need some rack time after I get back in, but I'll ping you after that, huh?" She kisses me once more on the mouth. "Make sure you brush your teeth first, though. That cycler paste is nasty."

She pats me once on the cheek, picks up her tray, and goes.

I SHOULDN'T BE nervous about going to see Marshall. I mean, he's not likely to have me killed today. Especially lately, I can't always say that.

Anyway, he may be our supreme commander, but I've known Marshall longer than I've known anyone else on Niflheim other than Berto. He was the first person to greet me when my shuttle docked at the orbital assembly plant where they were putting the finishing touches on the *Drakkar,* two days after my interview with Gwen Johansen and three days after Darius Blank's minion made me spend the longest thirty seconds of my life staring into the face of Satan.

Well, *greet* might be a strong word for what Marshall did. He was definitely there, though.

In all fairness to him, I probably didn't make a very good first impression. I'd never experienced free fall before the shuttle's gravitics cut out for the approach to the station. I'd seen vids of people in orbit, of course. You couldn't spend five minutes on the entertainment nets without seeing advertisements for the orbital resorts with tourists in wing suits playing zero-g handball or some damn thing. I always assumed it would be kind of relaxing—like floating in the ocean, but without having to worry about getting eaten by a kraken.

The thing is, though, it's not called free float. It's called free *fall*.

The second the gravitic field shut down, my stomach climbed up into my throat, my heart started pounding so hard I could feel it in my fingertips, and my lizard brain let me know in no uncertain terms that, visual evidence aside, we were dropping like rain from a clear blue sky, and we were definitely, definitely about to die.

I didn't lose it like a few of my fellow passengers did. I didn't scream, I didn't start flailing around, and I didn't need to use the vacuum mask they provided in the seat back for folks who couldn't keep their lunches down. I was okay. I definitely wasn't *good*, though, and by the time we'd docked and I'd made my way through the air lock and into the arrivals lounge, I was drenched in sweat and trembling.

I probably looked like a morphine addict two days into withdrawal—and that's the first impression Commander Marshall got of me.

Marshall was in the lounge waiting for us, floating by the viewport opposite the air lock, staring down at the night side of Midgard as it spun past five hundred klicks below. He waited until the last of the dozen would-be colonists from the shuttle had drifted into the lounge and the air lock's inner door had clanged shut behind her to acknowledge us. I could see right away that we were in the presence of someone who thought of himself as In Charge of Things. From his jet-black tight-fade haircut to his perpetually clenched jaw to the fact that he somehow managed to look like he had a metal rod for a spine even in free fall, he was almost a parody of the sort of cold-eyed, combat-hardened military man that Midgard hadn't ever actually had or needed.

It took me three years and two reincarnations to realize that his whole aspect was ten percent genuine priggishness, ten percent insecurity, and eighty percent overcompensation for the fact that, as designated ground commander, he may as well have been cargo for the entirety of the transit.

"Well," Marshall said, and kicked off the floor toward us. He caught himself with one hand on a grab bar set into the ceiling, then drifted down to more or less stand in front of me. "Welcome to Himmel Station. This will be your home until the *Drakkar* is cleared for boarding. My name is Hieronymus Marshall, and I'll be in charge of this little expedition. Have any of you been off-planet before?" A half dozen hands went up. Marshall nodded. "Excellent. And how many of you others are trying desperately not to vomit right now?" Three hands went up, then a hesitant fourth. Marshall nodded again. "Yes, well. You'll get over that eventually. Or else you won't, I suppose. Either way, you're here for the duration, as they say."

"Sir?"

It was one of the vomiters. Marshall turned to look at him.

"Yes?"

"Dugan, sir. Biology. When—" He belched, then grimaced and swallowed. "Ugh . . . when will they be transferring up our personal effects? They wouldn't let us bring them onto the shuttle."

Marshall gave him a tight smile. "They will not be, unfortunately. Mass, as you can probably imagine, is a bit of an issue on a trip of this sort. As a result, we've made the decision to forbid the transfer of personal items." That got a round of groans from the group, but Marshall cut it off with a wave. "None of that, please. I promise you'll be given everything you need, and I think you'll find there's little need for knickknacks on a beachhead colony." His eyes swept across us. "Any other questions?"

I raised my hand. This was the first of several mistakes I made in my early days as a colonist.

"Yes," Marshall said. "You are?"

"Mickey Barnes," I said. "They told us we had a thirty-kilo personal allowance."

His smile became slightly tighter, and significantly less of a smile.

"As I said, Mr. Barnes, the decision was made to rescind that allowance."

"Nobody told us that," I said. "I need some of the stuff that I left in my bag."

Marshall was definitely not smiling anymore. "Mr. Barnes," he said. "When we are fully loaded, there will be one hundred and ninety-eight colonists and crew onboard the *Drakkar*. If each of them brought aboard thirty kilos of figurines and hand lotion and whatnot, that would increase the mass of the ship by nearly six thousand kilograms."

"I know," I said. "I can do math. I just—"

"Do you know how much energy is required to accelerate six thousand kilograms to point-nine c?"

"Um . . ." I said.

The smile came back. "Not so good at math after all, hmm?"

"It doesn't matter," I said. "Six thousand kilos can't be more than a rounding error in the mass of the ship."

"It does matter," Marshall said. "The answer, in case you were wondering, is just a bit more than four times ten to the twenty-third joules, and a similar amount of energy is needed at journey's end to decelerate back to rest. Physics is cruel, Mr. Barnes, and the antimatter that fuels starships is heinously expensive. The mass of the *Drakkar* has been reduced to the absolute minimum necessary to allow it to keep you alive for the nine years or so that it will take us to reach our destination, at astronomical expense to the government of Midgard. I assume you are aware that ninety percent of your fellow colonists are traveling in the form of frozen embryos, are you not?"

"Yes, but—"

"Why do you suppose that is, Mr. Barnes? Do you think it's because we all long to spend our waning years as nursemaids to a horde of children?" He paused and looked at me, as if he expected an answer. After it became clear that I wasn't going to give him one, he went on. "No, it is not. It's because embryos are light, and fully formed adult humans are heavy. Do you know what else is heavy? Food, Mr. Barnes. Once you see what your calorie ration is going to be for the remainder of your natural life, you may begin to wish that we had allocated those six thousand kilos to increasing our agricultural capacity. Personally, if we had that quantity of mass to spare, I would be much more inclined to allocate it to another seventy or eighty colonists. In any case, however, I'm sure we can all come up with hundreds of more productive ways to allocate any additional mass we might carry than to your *luggage*."

I opened my mouth to point out that unlike another seventy colonists, my *luggage* wouldn't require increasing the ship's stores of food, water, oxygen, and living space by forty percent, and more importantly that if somebody had told me that my *luggage* would not be coming aboard with me I could have shoved my tablet and a couple of memory chips, which was all I really wanted, into a pocket or something before boarding the shuttle.

I'm not completely stupid, though. The look on Marshall's face made me decide that maybe silent protest was the way to go.

"By the way," Marshall said, "I didn't quite catch your function, Mr. Barnes."

"My what?"

"Your function, son. Mr. Dugan here is a biologist. What are you?"

This was where my initial mistake compounded itself. I grinned. "I'm your Expendable, sir."

Marshall did not return my smile. His face twisted into the kind of scowl I was used to seeing on people who'd just bitten into something rotten, or maybe stepped barefoot into a pile of dung.

"I suppose I should have guessed," he said. He kicked up to the grab bar again, pushed off with both hands toward an exit at the far side of the lounge, then executed a neat midair somersault that left him kicking off the floor and into a smooth swimmer's glide.

"There obviously aren't sufficient individual quarters available on the station to accommodate all of the mission's colonists and crew," he said over his shoulder as the exit door slid open. "There are, however, slings set up in many of the common spaces. Find one. That's your home until we can board the *Drakkar*."

He slipped through the door, and it slid shut behind him.

"Wow," Dugan said when he was gone. "What was that about?"

"Commander Marshall is a Natalist," a tall, dark-haired woman who'd been hanging back by the air lock said.

Dugan barked out a short, sharp laugh. "Seriously?" He turned to look at me. "You're screwed, friend."

I looked from Dugan to the woman and back. "I don't get it," I said. "What's a Natalist?"

"They're a cult," Dugan said.

"They're not a cult," the woman said. She kicked off the wall with almost as much dexterity as Marshall had shown, caught herself on the grab bar, and plopped down in front of me. "They're a serious religion, and Commander Marshall is a serious believer.

I checked his digital profile. I checked out everyone in Command before I signed on to this gig. Didn't you?"

I didn't feel like this was necessarily the best time to get into the fact that I'd been too busy fleeing from gangsters with torture machines to worry about being a social media detective, so I just shook my head.

She laughed. "You've got to be kidding. You realize these people are going to own us for the rest of our lives, right? You didn't even bother to look into who they are?"

"No," I said. "No, I did not."

Dugan laughed again. I had already decided that I didn't like his laugh.

"He wouldn't have," he said. "You were conscripted, right? What were you, a prisoner or something?"

"What? No, I wasn't a prisoner, and no, I wasn't conscripted. I was *selected* for the mission, just like you were."

"Right," Dugan said. "Selected, conscripted, whatever. The point is, you didn't have a choice."

I shook my head. "You're not listening. I had a choice. I walked into the recruitment office two days ago, all on my own. A lady named Gwen interviewed me. She said I was an excellent candidate, and they were very happy to have me."

They both stared at me like I'd grown a second head.

"You're kidding," Dugan said.

"No," I said. "I'm not."

"If you don't mind my asking," the woman said, "what the hell were you thinking?"

I considered just spilling it about Darius Blank then, but good sense stopped me at the last second. I didn't need the people I was going to be spending the rest of my life with thinking I was some kind of criminal.

"Doesn't matter," I said. "The point is, I volunteered, I've never been to prison, and no, I did not do a social media search on anyone before I signed on."

"I didn't either," Dugan said. "This is Midgard's first colony expedition, right? I assumed everyone involved would be the best and the brightest. I can't believe they put a Natalist in charge of the whole show."

"It's not a big deal," the woman said, then turned to look at me. "Well, not for anyone but this guy, anyway." She gave me a sad look, then held her hand out to Dugan. "I'm Bree, by the way. I'm with Agriculture. I'd guess we'll be working together."

The rest of the new arrivals had drifted away by then, presumably looking for a sling to call their own. As Bree and Dugan smiled and shook, I began to suspect that this whole escape-the-planet thing might not have been as solid a plan as I'd hoped.

"Look," I said. "I don't mean to be stupid, but could one of you please explain what Marshall's religion has to do with me?"

Bree pivoted back toward me. Her expression said that Dugan was much more interesting, probably because she'd concluded that there was something seriously wrong with me and that I was starting to get on her nerves.

"One of the prime doctrines of the Natalist Church," she said, "is the belief in the sanctity of the unitary soul."

"Uh . . ."

"They don't like backups," Dugan said. "They believe it's one soul to a body, and once your original body dies, your soul is dead as well."

"Right," Bree said. "Which means that a bio-printed body with a personality imprinted from backup is, in fact, a soulless monster."

"Yeah," Dugan said. "An abomination, you know?"

"Not fully human."

Dugan nodded. "Not human at all, really."

"Huh," I said. "That's . . ."

"I know," Bree said. "Unfortunate."

"But hey," Dugan said, "just because you're the Expendable doesn't mean you've been expended yet, right? I mean, you're still the original you right now, aren't you?"

"Well, yeah," I said. "I just signed on to the expedition two days ago. I'm not even sure how this whole backup thing is supposed to work. For now, at least, I'm still in the same body I was born in."

"Great," Dugan said, and clapped me on the shoulder. "All you have to do to stay on Marshall's good side is keep it that way."

That was some solid advice, brother.

Can't imagine why I didn't think to follow it.

I GENERALLY TRY not to be late for things, particularly when lateness might threaten my food supply. I'm not a big fan of early either, though, and that goes double when the thing I'm early for is a dressing-down from Hieronymus Marshall. I take my time walking the corridors, actually stop to chat with a couple of people along the way, then loiter in the hallway outside Marshall's office door until the chronometer at the edge of my field of view hits 10:29 before knocking.

"Come."

The door swings open. Marshall sits behind a squat metal-and-plastic desk. He's leaning forward in his chair, elbows on the armrests, hands folded across his belly. Berto is sitting across from him, turned half around to see me.

"Close the door," Marshall says. "Take a seat."

I pull a chair up next to Berto and sit. Marshall stares us both down wordlessly for a painfully long time.

"So—" Berto begins finally, but Marshall cuts him off with a glare.

"You," he says. "Barnes. What iteration are you?"

"Uh," I say. "Eight?"

He raises one eyebrow in question. "You don't sound sure of this."

"It's not stamped on the back of my neck, sir, and I don't remember most of the dying. I only know I'm Eight because you guys tell me so."

"You remember coming out of the tank, do you not?"

I glance over at Berto. He's staring straight ahead.

"Not really, sir. I don't generally regain consciousness for a few hours afterward. Mostly what I remember is waking up in my bed and feeling really hungover."

Marshall's face darkens, but his expression doesn't change.

"Considering that you have no access to alcohol here on Niflheim, Mr. Barnes, I think we can take it as a given that such experiences are more likely to indicate reboots than the results of three-day benders, wouldn't you say?"

I have a smart-ass answer to that, but I'm sensing that this probably isn't the time.

"Yes, sir," I say. "I believe that's a fair assumption."

"So how many times has that happened, Barnes?"

"Seven times, sir."

"So you are in fact the eighth iteration of Mickey Barnes?"

"Yes, sir," I say. "I am the eighth."

Marshall stares at me for a while longer, then turns his eyes to Berto. "Gomez. Why is this man the eighth iteration of Mr. Barnes?"

"Well, sir," he says. "Protocol states that we have to have a functioning Expendable at all times."

"And?"

"And as of last night, the seventh iteration was no longer functional. Therefore, per protocol, I submitted a request to initiate the production of Mickey8."

"Thank you," Marshall says. "That was very officious, Gomez. You actually managed to sound as if you gave a shit about protocol for a second there."

"Sir—" Berto begins, but Marshall shakes his head.

"Save it, son. Just explain to me, please, in normal words that don't sound as if you pulled them from a field manual, exactly how you managed to flush seventy-five kilos of protein and calcium down the toilet last night."

I'm actually only about seventy-one kilos, and most of that is water, which we have more than enough of piled up in drifts outside, but this doesn't seem like the right moment to raise the point.

"Right," Berto says. "Well, sir . . ."

Marshall leans forward, props his elbow on the desk, and rests his chin on one palm as his eyebrows creep up toward his hairline. Berto clears his throat. This may be the most nervous I've ever seen him.

"As I stated in my reboot request, Mickey was lost at approximately—"

"The seventh iteration of Mr. Barnes, you mean."

"Yes, sir. Mickey7. He was lost at approximately twenty-five-thirty last night, while exploring a crevasse roughly eight kilometers southwest of the main dome. This exploration was in compliance with your standing orders regarding reconnaissance of the colony's immediate surroundings and surveillance of the local fauna. After I had confirmed that his body was not recoverable—"

"Confirmed how?"

I glance over at Berto. He keeps his eyes straight ahead. This should be good.

"Sir?"

"I thought that was pretty clear," Marshall says. "How did you confirm that the body could not be recovered?"

"Well," Berto says, and then shoots me a quick glance.

"Don't look at me," I say. "I was the body, remember?"

"If this is making you uncomfortable, Barnes," Marshall says, "you can wait outside until I'm finished with this line of inquiry."

I shake my head. "Oh no. I'm as interested in hearing this as you are."

Marshall's eyes shift back to Berto. "So?"

"Well," Berto says, "he fell down a hole."

Marshall leans back in his chair and folds his arms across his chest.

"He what?"

"He fell down a hole," Berto says. "An extremely deep one. By the time he stopped moving, the signal from his transponder was practically nil."

"Practically? So you could have located him."

"I mean . . ."

"You could have located him," Marshall says, "which means that you could have retrieved him. Is this not correct?"

"Huh," I say. "That sounds pretty reasonable to me."

Marshall and Berto shoot me simultaneous glares. Berto clears his throat and tries again.

"In my judgment, sir, it would not have been safe to attempt a landing in the area where Mickey went down."

"I see," Marshall says. "And yet, you felt it was safe enough to drop him there in the first place. Is that correct?"

"Yeah," I say. "What was up with that?"

Marshall jabs a finger in my direction. "Quiet, Barnes. I'll deal with you when I'm finished with Gomez." He turns back to Berto. "Look, son, your orders are to explore the dome's immediate surroundings, and to make observations of the things you've taken to calling *creepers* where and when it is prudent to do so. However, I expect you to use some damned judgment in your execution of those orders. In particular, if in your estimation there is a reasonable probability that the Expendable may be killed in the course of carrying out his duties, I expect you to make provision for the recovery and recycling of his body. Do I make myself clear?"

Nine years ago I might have been offended at the clear inference that the problem was not the fact that Berto got me killed, but rather that he didn't put sufficient effort into dredging up my corpse afterward. At this point, though, I would have been surprised if Marshall hadn't put it that way.

Berto opens his mouth to reply, but Marshall's eyes narrow, and I guess Berto thinks better of it, because his jaw snaps closed again and he nods mutely.

Marshall turns to me. "Now, Barnes. What do you have to say about all of this?"

"Me, sir? I'm afraid I don't have any opinions on this matter at all. If you'll recall, I just came out of the tank, and Seven apparently hadn't uploaded for several weeks prior to his death last night. I have no idea what the two of you have been talking about."

"Hmm," Marshall says. "Yes, I suppose that's true. I forget sometimes that you're simply a construct."

Ordinarily I'd argue that point—but again, this really doesn't seem like the time for it.

"In any case," Marshall says, "I'm sure you're both aware that our Agricultural Section has been having great difficulty getting virtually anything to grow properly in this environment, and that as a result we are currently operating on a very thin margin, calorie-wise. Your activities of the past several weeks have permanently removed nearly three hundred thousand kilocalories from our energy budget. Unless and until we are able to bring our agricultural base up to full production, this loss will necessitate a further reduction in our calorie rations." He pauses then, and leans forward again with his elbows planted on his desk. "I'm sure you'd agree that it is only equitable that the two of you should bear the brunt of this reduction."

"Sir—" Berto begins, but Marshall shakes his head.

"No, Gomez. I don't want to hear it. Both of your ration cards are hereby permanently docked by twenty percent."

"But—"

"I said," Mashall grates, enunciating each word, "I do not want to hear it." He stares Berto down, then turns to me. "Do you have anything further, Barnes?"

"Well," I say, "to be honest, sir, it's not clear to me why I should be sanctioned for the failure to recover my own corpse."

Marshall stares me down for a long five seconds, then blinks and says, "Allow me to rephrase my question. Do you have anything further that is not simply an inane bit of smart-assery?"

I do, but it's pretty clear there's no real point, so I shake my head and say, "No, sir."

"Good," Marshall says. "Perhaps your growling bellies will remind you to take better care of colony assets in the future. Dismissed."

"So," Berto says when we're safely out of Marshall's earshot, "how does it feel to be a *colony asset*?"

"Good question," I say. "Here's one for you: How does it feel to be a lying sack of shit?"

He stops walking. I wheel around to face him. He actually manages to look hurt.

"Come on, Mickey. That's not fair."

"You told me I got eaten by creepers, Berto."

He looks away. "Yeah. That wasn't exactly true."

"Exactly? It wasn't true at all. You left me to die down there, didn't you?"

A woman from Bio scoots past us in the corridor, clearly doing her best to ignore whatever is going on between us. When you spend nine years crammed into an ark together like rabbits in a hutch, you learn to do whatever you can to grant one another at least a tiny modicum of privacy.

"Please," Berto says. "Keep your voice down, huh?"

"Fine."

I turn and start walking again. He hesitates, then hurries to catch up.

"Look," he says. "I'm sorry. Seriously. I should have told you the truth."

"Yeah," I say. "You definitely should have."

"Right," he says. "That's on me—but I did *not* leave you to die, Mickey. That fall you took must have been at least a hundred meters. By the time you hit bottom, you were already dead. I wasn't going to risk my ass for Marshall's seventy-five kilos of protein, but if there had been any chance of getting you out of there alive, I would have done it. You know that, right?"

Good God, I want to hit him right now. He was sitting right there when Nasha said she was in contact with me after the fall last night. It's like he thinks that spouting bullshit sincerely enough will make it true. If it weren't for the fact that he can't know that I know exactly what he actually did, and also that he's taller, faster, and stronger than I am and could probably break my neck like a chicken's, I might actually do it.

"Yeah," I say. "I know. You'd never leave your best friend to die, Berto. I mean, you might leave one *iteration* of a *colony asset* to die. What's the harm in that? If a *friend* was in trouble, though? You'd definitely be all over it."

He grabs my shoulder, pulls me up short, and spins me around. He lets me go, though, raises both hands in surrender, and takes a step back when he sees my face.

"Woah," he says. "I don't know what's going on here, Mickey, but you need to get a grip. It sucks that you went down last night, but come on, in your line of work, that's just part of the job, right? I mean, Marshall's killed you deliberately at least three times now. I don't remember you getting all pissy about any of those. What are you so worked up about now?"

I close my eyes, take a deep breath, and let it out slowly. "I am angry, Berto, because I live an extremely messed-up life. Every so often I wake up in my bed, hungover and covered in goo, and I realize that something horrible just happened to me, and I don't have any memory of what it was, or why it happened, or what I could possibly do to prevent it from happening again. And when that happens, I trust you and Nasha to fill me in, to tell me what happened. I have to trust you, because I have no way to remember this stuff for myself. And now I know for a certain fact that you have lied to me about what happened at least once, and that leads me to wonder how many other times you've lied to me. Can you understand that?"

Maybe that got to him, because now he can't meet my eyes.

"Yeah," he says softly. "I understand that. I'm sorry, Mickey. Honestly, I am. I never thought about it that way."

He actually seems sincere. Maybe he wouldn't be such a terrible poker player after all.

"Yeah, well," I say. "Maybe you should have."

"Maybe." He looks up, and breaks into a grin. "Tell you what—next time I'll see if I can get video of whatever takes you out. If I can, I'll show it to Nine as soon as he comes out of the tank."

I don't want to let this go just yet—but, lying sack of shit or not, he is more or less my best friend.

"That's really thoughtful, you asshole."

He reaches out then and pulls me into a bear hug with those goddamned gangly monkey arms.

"Seriously," he says. "I'm sorry I lied to you, Mickey. I won't let it happen again."

"Yeah," I mutter into his chest. "I'll just bet you won't."

IT OCCURS TO me at this point that I'm not painting Berto in a particularly positive light, and that you may be wondering why I was ever friends with this guy in the first place. The short answer is that I've always believed it's important to accept the people in your life for what they are. There's no such thing as a perfect friend, any more than there's any such thing as a perfect anything, and if you slag everyone in your life for their many and varied failings, you're going to miss appreciating the good stuff they bring to the table.

As an example, during my last couple of years in school, I had a friend named Ben Aslan. Ben was a good noodle. He was smart enough to get me through two semesters of astrophysics despite my complete lack of mathematical aptitude, funny enough to get me suspended for two days during twelfth form for cracking up during our late vice administrator's funeral, and loyal enough to stick around and take a beating with me when I got on the wrong side of a bunch of extremely drunk older guys at a Copper Fist concert the summer after we graduated.

Ben was also unbelievably, almost pathologically, cheap.

The Aslans owned a controlling interest in the company that held the intercity shipping franchise for the entire planet. His dad dipped in and out of the list of the twenty-five wealthiest people on Midgard. Ben himself owned a flitter, a ground car, a beach house, and a guy who cleaned up his dormitory room for him. Despite that, in all the time I knew him, I don't think Ben Aslan ever picked up a check. He didn't have implants, because he said he was afraid that if he did, somebody might cut his eye out to get access to his trust fund, and he never seemed to remember to bring a phone along when we went out because why would he? If he needed to talk to someone, he had people to do it for him. The upshot was that when the check came around, he'd smile and shrug and promise to pick up the next one.

This went on for years.

Why did I put up with it? Why did I, a kid who never had more than twenty credits in his account at any given time, buy gallons of beer and mountains of food for the richest person I'd ever met? Simple, really. I knew who Ben was, and I accepted it. I added up the benefits of having him in my life, deducted the annoyance of having to pay for everything anytime we went anywhere, and decided that on the balance, he was a net positive. Once I'd made that decision, I quit worrying about the checks. It wasn't worth it.

I guess it's kind of the same with Berto, except instead of cheaping out on restaurant tabs, he occasionally leaves me to freeze to death in a hole and then lies about it later. That's who he is. Everything's easier if you can just accept that and move on.

WHEN I GET back to my rack, I find Eight curled up in my bed, sound asleep. I think about letting him be—tank funk is rough—but I'm tired too, and we've got things to discuss. I latch the door, then grab the top sheet and yank it off of him. He's naked.

I make a mental note to change my sheets.

Eight lifts his head up and blinks at me, then grabs at the sheet and tries to pull it back over him. It's then that I notice that he's got a pressure wrap on his left wrist.

"Hey," I say. "What happened to your hand?"

He shoots me a withering look. "Nothing, idiot. We need to

look like the same person now, right? You can't take the wrap off of your wrist, so I needed to put one on mine."

"It's not purple."

He looks down at his hand, then up at me. "What?"

"Your hand," I say. "It's wrapped, but it's not purple. Anyone who looks at it closely will be able to see that you're not really hurt."

"If anybody's looking closely," he says, "we're probably already dead."

He flops back onto the pillow and pulls the sheet back up to his chin. I sigh, and yank it off again.

"Sorry," I say. "Time to wake up. We've got a few issues that we need to go over."

He sits up, rubs his knuckles into his eyes, and pulls the sheet up to his waist.

"Seriously? You know I just came out of the tank, right? Don't we usually get a day to recover?"

I sit down on the edge of the bed. "Yeah, we won't get a work detail today—which is a good thing, because exactly how we're going to handle our duty cycles is one of the things we're going to need to figure out. Only one of us can be out and about at a time if we don't want Marshall shoving us both down the corpse hole."

Eight yawns, rubs his eyes again, and looks at me. A smile slowly spreads across his face. "Hey, that's a good point. This could actually work out pretty well, couldn't it? Only having to pull half duty isn't so bad, right?"

"Yeah," I say. "As long as our shifts are getting seconded out to Agriculture or Engineering, we can share. What happens the next time Marshall decides he needs someone to scrub out the antimatter reaction chamber, though?"

His smile fades. "That is definitely gonna happen at some point, isn't it?"

"It is. We should probably figure out how we're going to handle it ahead of time, no?"

He shrugs. "Seems pretty obvious to me. I shouldn't have come out of the tank until you checked out. Ergo, if we want to set things right, you should be the one who takes on the next suicide mission."

That doesn't seem obvious to me. I'm about to explain to him exactly why his argument is utter bullshit, but . . .

I actually can't come up with a good reason why he isn't right.

"Fine," I say. "If and when Marshall comes up with an actual suicide mission for us—I mean something like what he did to Three—I'll fall on the sword. I'm not taking every hazardous job, though. If he sends us out on another recon mission, or posts us to the perimeter, or sends us up in the flitter with Berto again, we're throwing hands for it."

He squints at me, head tilted to one side, and for a second I think he's going to try to argue the point. Finally, though, he just shrugs and says, "Yeah, fair enough."

"Good," I say. "I guess we can play it by ear the next time a summons comes through."

"Anyway," he says, "until and unless one of us goes down, living on half rations is definitely going to suck."

"Yeah," I say. "About that."

"About what? Rations, or duty?"

"Rations," I say. "That meeting with Marshall didn't exactly go the way I was hoping."

His face falls. "Tell me."

"He cut our ration by twenty percent."

Eight groans.

"I know," I say. "This would be bad even if there were only one of us. As it is, the next however long is gonna be really, really rough."

He leans back against the wall, tilts his head back, and closes his eyes.

"You think? This is a disaster, Seven. I just came out of the tank. I am literally starving to death right now. If I don't get some calories in my belly, I'm liable to bite your arm off and eat it while you're sleeping."

I run my hands back through my hair. They come away with a light sheen of oil, which reminds me that I haven't showered in almost a week.

"Did you get anything to eat this morning?"

He opens his eyes, looks away, and scowls. "If you want to call it that. I grabbed a paste-and-slurry smoothie on my way past the caf."

"Nice. How many kcal did you burn?"

"Six hundred, I think."

"Yeah," I say. "Me too. That leaves us another four hundred total for the day."

"Good freaking lord," he moans. "Two hundred apiece?"

I breathe in deep, hold it, and then let it out. "You can have it."

His eyes widen. "Are you serious?"

"I'm giving you two hundred kcal of slurry," I say. "Don't make this a thing."

"What about tomorrow?"

"Don't push it. Tomorrow we're back to fifty-fifty."

He sighs. "Yeah, that's fair. In fact, it's more than fair. Thanks, Seven."

I clap one hand to his knee. "No problem. It's probably the least I can do after you decided not to kill me this morning."

"Yeah," he says. "That's true. That was pretty magnanimous of me, honestly. Sure you don't want to give me the whole card for tomorrow?"

I give his leg an almost-painful squeeze before letting go.

"Again," I say, "don't push it. I'm pretty sure the next time one of us gets a full day's rations, it'll be because the other one is dead."

He lies back and folds his hands behind his head. "There's something to look forward to."

"Yeah." I'm about to go on about how at some point scrubbing out the reaction chamber might not seem like such a bad idea when I remember my conversation in the caf. "Hey—while I'm thinking about it, did you happen to run into Berto on your way back up here?"

"No. Why?"

"I saw him in the caf this morning. He sort of implied that you did. I think he's got some suspicions about us."

He shrugs. "Well, if we have to tell him, we have to tell him. It'll probably gross him out, but it's not like he can go crying to Command. He's as much to blame for this as anyone."

"Truth." I start to say something more, but have to stifle a yawn. Eight's eyes are already closed.

I give him a nudge. "Scoot over, huh?"

He slides over to the edge of the bed. I pull off my boots and lie down beside him. It's a little weird sharing a bed with myself, but I guess we'll have to get used to it.

I'm just drifting off when my ocular flashes.

<Command1>:We need you at the main lock immediately, Barnes. We have a problem.

My heart gives a sudden lurch. Did Berto slink back to Marshall's office and turn us in?

No. If Command knew about us, they wouldn't have just pinged me. They would have sent Security up here with cable ties and burners. I turn my head to look at Eight. His eyes are still closed.

"I think they want you, friend," he says.

I sit up. "This is a summons, Eight."

"Yeah," he says. "If it's a terminal job, it's on you, right? If it's just some scut work, that should be on you today too, because I just came out of the tank."

"What if it's one of those in-betweens? Are we throwing hands?"

"Nah," he says. "I think you owe me this one."

He rolls onto his side and pulls the sheet up over his shoulder. I waste a few seconds glaring at the back of his head, then swing my legs over the edge of the bed, sit up, and pull my boots back on. He's already snoring when I latch the door behind me.

I DO A lot of things around the dome. I'm not attached to any particular section, so they generally rotate me every couple of days to wherever they need a bit of extra grunt labor. I've tended to the rabbit hutches for Agriculture. I've stood sentry for Security. Once I even filled in for Marshall's admin while he took a sick day that I found out later was actually the result of his having made an attempt at homemade booze that went really, really wrong. Those jobs, though, were just random assignments from the semiautonomous system that runs HR for the colony. When I get a direct summons from Command, it's not because they need somebody to help move boxes. It's because they need me to do my actual job.

What my actual job *is* was impressed on me pretty clearly right from the jump, beginning with my first day cycle on Himmel Station. I'd managed to find a bathroom by then, and after a couple of painful and messy errors had more or less figured out how peeing works in zero-g. I'd found the room where they were handing out food packets. I'd even found a sling to call my own, strung up with forty or so others in what appeared to be a conference room.

The smell wasn't great, but I was already starting to get used to it. All in all, I felt like I was settling into my new life pretty well.

I was napping, wrapped in my sling, finally almost able to imagine that I was floating rather than falling, when something hard and pointy dug itself into my ribs. I batted at it, which sent the sling spinning on its long axis. I opened my eyes to see floor, then wall, then ceiling, then the person who had poked me. She was tall, dark-skinned, and hairless, dressed in the shapeless gray jumpsuit that all the permanent station personnel wore. She reached out to grab me, braced her feet against the floor, and stopped my spin.

"You're Barnes, right?"

I blinked up at her. "Maybe. Who's asking?"

She grinned. "I'm Jemma. Get up. It's time to get to work."

FOR ALMOST ALL of my stay on Himmel Station, I liked Jemma. She was an excellent teacher. She was funny, and kind, and weirdly thoughtful. When we had morning sessions, she brought me bulbs of hot chai. When I had trouble picking something up, she slowed down, backed up, and repeated herself until she was sure I understood. If at any time during this process she got it into her head that I was a dimwit, she made a point not to ever let it show.

That first day, we started with the schematics for the *Drakkar*'s engine systems. I learned where the antimatter was stored, how it was contained, where they kept the reactants, how they brought the two together, and (this was the part Jemma emphasized) what would happen if any of these components broke down.

"We can skip a breakdown in the antimatter containment unit," she said. "That problem solves itself."

We were sitting across from one another at a card table in what looked to be a disused storage closet. Jemma gave me a half smile and waited. After five seconds or so, her face fell.

"Aren't you going to ask me how it does that?"

I rolled my eyes. "By killing us all?"

"Yes," she said. "But I was going to say it in a much funnier way."

I sighed. "Why do I need to know about any of this? We'll have engineers, right? If they're all dead, I don't think whatever you can cram into my head in the next two weeks is going to make much difference. I like history. I can tell you who Wernher von Braun was, but that's about my limit when it comes to propulsion tech. I barely passed high-energy physics in school, and that was a long time ago."

"I'm not trying to turn you into an engineer," she said. "The *Drakkar* will carry a fully redundant complement of propulsion specialists. They'll tell you exactly what needs to be done if the need arises—but time will likely be short if it comes to that, and things will go much faster if you already know the basics."

"And if something does go wrong, they'll need my help to fix it because . . ."

Her smile disappeared. "Because an hour after shutdown, the neutron flux in the combustion chamber is still high enough to provide a lethal dose even through full combat armor in less than sixty seconds—and if it comes to that, trust me, you will not be wearing full combat armor. That shit is expensive."

"Right," I said. "I didn't mean they'd crawl into the engines themselves. Who does that? I meant they'd use a drone."

She shook her head. "Drones are subject to damage from high-energy particles, just like you are. In fact, you'd be surprised how much longer a human will last in a stream of heavy particles than a mechanical. You may be dead for all practical purposes after sixty seconds in there, but it will take your body an hour or more to figure that out, and you can be doing useful work for that entire time. A drone in that environment will shut down in under a minute—and once you're away from Midgard's industrial base, a damaged drone will be a lot more difficult to replace than you will. Your official title is *Mission Expendable,* Mickey. Part of my job over the next twelve days or so is to make sure you really understand what that means."

I think that's probably the point where I started liking her slightly less.

WE DIDN'T ONLY talk about schematics and radiation poisoning, Jemma and I. When it was pretty clear that my head was full up with technical data for the moment, we switched over to philosophy, which was much more my speed.

Turns out that people have been poking around the periphery of what has become the central question of my life for a long time. That first day, after we were finished talking about the many different ways I could irradiate myself into oblivion, Jemma told me about the Ship of Theseus.

"Imagine," she said, "that one day Theseus sets out to sail around the world."

"Okay," I said. "I know I should know this, but who's Theseus?"

"An old Earth hero," she said. "Seriously old school—from maybe three thousand years before the Diaspora."

"Huh. And he's sailing around the world?"

"Right," she said. "He's sailing around the world in a wooden ship. As he goes, parts of the ship get damaged or wear out, and he has to replace them. Years later, when he finally comes home, every single board and timber of the original ship has been replaced. So. Is this, or is this not, the same ship that he departed in?"

"That's dumb," I said. "Of course it is."

"Okay," she said. "What if the ship is destroyed in a storm, and he has to rebuild it all at once before sailing on? Is it the same ship then?"

"No," I said. "That's totally different. If he has to rebuild the entire ship, that's Ship of Theseus II, the Sequel."

She leaned forward then, elbows on the table. "Really? Why? What difference does it make if he replaces every component one by one, or if he replaces them all at once?"

I opened my mouth to answer, but then realized that I had no idea what to say.

"This is the key to accepting this job, Mickey. *You* are the Ship of Theseus. We all are. There is not a single living cell in my body that was alive and a part of me ten years ago, and the same is true for you. We're constantly being rebuilt, one board at a time. If you actually take on this job, you'll probably be rebuilt all at once at some point, but at the end of the day, it's really no different, is it? When an Expendable takes a trip to the tank, he's just doing in one go what his body would naturally do over the course of time anyway. As long as memory is preserved, he hasn't really died. He's just undergone an unusually rapid remodeling."

I DON'T WANT to make it sound like my training was all engine schematics and Theseuses. Some of it was actually fun. Jemma taught me the basics of handling a linear accelerator, for example. I couldn't actually fire a real one on the station, but she ran me through a pretty realistic simulation where I got to fight space zombies, and when I finally did get a chance to use the real thing years later, it wasn't much different. She showed me how to get in and out of a vacuum suit. She showed me how to assemble a full set of combat armor. On Day Six she actually took me outside, and we clambered around the hull of the station for an hour and practiced using recoilless wrenches to tighten and loosen bolts. I will never forget standing with her on the underside of the station and looking up to see the night side of Midgard rolling by.

"I know," Jemma said. "It's something, right?"

"That bright patch," I said. "That's Kiruna, right?"

"Yeah," she said. "You from there?"

I nodded. She couldn't see that through my mirrored visor, but she seemed to understand.

"And now you're leaving forever," she said. We hung there in silence for a while and watched Midgard swing by until Kiruna disappeared over the horizon. "I admire you guys," she said then. "The colonists, I mean. I don't understand you, but I admire you. I get the romance of it. I get that spreading humanity as widely as we can, making us as disaster-proof as we can, is the whole point of the Diaspora—but I could never just go."

I shrugged. "Yeah, well. Some of us are just born explorers, I guess."

Jemma gave an incredulous snort. I turned to look at her, but I couldn't see her face any more than she could see mine.

"I've trained Expendables before," she said. "We need them here on the station from time to time. They're usually pretty difficult to deal with. You're a pain in the ass, but ordinarily when I take them outside like this I'm worried they'll cut my tether and shove me into the void. Any idea why that would be?"

I sighed. "I know most Expendables are convicts," I said. "It's different, though, signing on to be an Expendable on Himmel Station. That's just agreeing to get killed every once in a while for no good reason. I signed on for a colony mission. Like you said, it's a romance thing, right?"

Jemma laughed. "Oh please," she said. "I talked to your friend. Gomez? The pilot? I know why you signed on to this mission."

"Oh," I said. "Um . . ."

She laughed again. "Don't worry, I'm not about to tell anybody important. Your reasons for going are probably at least as valid as his, or Marshall's, or any of the others'. I hope you know, though, that this is a permanent solution to a temporary problem."

"Isn't that what they say about suicide?"

She put a hand on my shoulder. "Come on, Mickey. Let's get back inside. We need to have a talk about John Locke."

MY FIRST BACKUP came on the morning of my twelfth day on Himmel Station. The physical part was pretty straightforward. They took a blood sample, snipped some skin from my belly, tapped my cerebrospinal fluid, and then stuck me into a scanner that spent three hours mapping out the distribution and chemical makeup of every cell in my body. Jemma was waiting for me when I came out.

"Hope you're having a good hair day," she said. "The way you look right now is exactly how you're going to look every time you come out of the tank for the rest of your life."

"Huh," I said. "This is a onetime thing?"

"Afraid so," she said. "That scanner draws an unbelievable amount of power, and the recon software will be running for almost a week now sorting out the information it extracted. Also, you just absorbed what under normal circumstances would be a problematic amount of radiation."

"Oh."

She grabbed a handhold and pushed off down the hall. I followed.

"Wait," I said when we reached our next stop. "What did you mean, that 'would be' a problematic amount of radiation?"

She gave me a sad half smile. "You'll see."

THE PERSONALITY BACKUP, which I've been repeating on a regular basis ever since then, was both simpler and stranger than the physical one. I sat in a chair, and a technician placed a helmet on my head. The outside was smooth and metallic. The inside was covered in dull-pointed spikes that pressed into my scalp and forehead.

"This is a squid array," the technician said. "It's a little uncomfortable, but it won't hurt you."

I later learned that a squid, in addition to being a surprisingly intelligent marine invertebrate from old Earth, is also a superconducting quantum interference device. I hope that means more to you than it did to me.

The tech was right that the backup process isn't painful. It is, however, profoundly weird. Routine backups are just updates. They take about an hour to get through. That first one, though, took almost eighteen, and it felt much longer. The backup process is like a fever dream. Bits and pieces of your past flit by, pictures and sounds and smells and sensations, all out of your control and all too fast to process. The thing I remember most vividly from that first upload is a close shot of my mother's face. She died joyriding in a flitter when I was eight, and I barely remembered what she looked like . . . but in that image she was young and vivid and beautiful, and when they finally took the helmet off of me, I was sobbing.

When that was done, Jemma took me to the officers' mess, got us a table, and told me to order whatever I wanted. When I asked what was going on, she gave me that sad smile again and said, "We're celebrating, Mickey. Today's your graduation."

"Really?" I said. "When's the ceremony?"

She looked away. "As soon as we're done here. Take your time."

I still remember that as one of the strangest hours of my life. The food was pretty good, considering that most of it was vat-grown and it was prepared in zero-g. The conversation was awkward, for reasons that I totally misunderstood. I knew the *Drakkar* was almost ready to begin loading. Believe it or not, I actually thought Jemma might be sad because she was going to miss me when I was gone.

When dinner was over and Jemma had settled up, I thought I'd head back to my sling to catch up on my sleep. I hadn't actually been awake for the entire time I'd been uploading, but I hadn't really been resting either. I wasn't tired, exactly—more like stretched out and worn thin, and not quite connected to reality anymore. Jemma caught my arm when I started down the corridor, though.

"No," she said. "Your graduation ceremony, remember?"

"Oh," I said. "I thought that was a joke."

She stared at me for a long few seconds, then shook her head and pushed off back down the corridor toward our closet. I shrugged, and followed.

"So," I SAID when she'd closed the door behind her. "Do I get a cap and gown, or what?"

I drifted closer to her.

I thought we were about to have sex.

Yes, I am exactly that stupid.

Jemma's face was as blank as a wooden mask. She reached into a pocket of her jumpsuit, and pulled out a shiny black . . . something . . . a little bigger than her hand.

"What's that?" I asked.

She held it up. It had a pistol grip and a snub nose with a white crystal tip. For the first time in almost two weeks, it felt like I was falling again.

"It's a burner," she said. "Low power, so it's safe to use on-station. It won't cut through metal, but it'll do a number on pretty much any kind of organic matter."

She held it by the nose and offered it to me. After a moment, I took it.

"See the red switch on the side of the grip? That's the safety," she said. "Slide it forward."

I did. The tip took on a dull yellow glow.

"Okay," she said. "It's armed. Careful with the trigger. It's that nub next to your index finger."

I turned the weapon over in my hand. "I don't understand," I said.

But then she gave me that sad look again, and I did.

"This is your graduation, Mickey. Time to prove that you understand what it means to be an Expendable."

I looked at her. She looked back.

"You're not serious," I said.

"You want this to be quick," she said. "Turn your head as far to the side as you can, and press the tip against the soft spot just behind your ear. Try to angle the weapon slightly upward. It's set for a fan beam. If you do it right, you'll take out your entire medulla oblongata and a good chunk of your cerebellum with one shot. I promise, you won't feel a thing. If you miss, I might have to do cleanup for you. Neither one of us wants that."

"Jemma—"

"This isn't really your graduation ceremony," she said. "It's more like your final exam. If you don't do this, you'll be on a shuttle back down to Midgard in the morning, and I'll have to start over with a conscript tomorrow. Neither one of us wants that either. I'm sorry, Mickey, but this is what you signed on for. Immortality comes with a price."

I thought about it. I thought about going back to Midgard, back to my shitty apartment and starvation subsidy. I thought about telling my friends that I wasn't going with the *Drakkar* after all.

I thought about Darius Blank's torture machine. "It's just like going to sleep, right?" I said. "I do this, and I wake up in my sling, good as new?"

"Right," she said. "A little hungover, maybe, but yeah."

She smiled. I sighed, looked away, and put the burner to my head.

"Like this?"

"Sure," she said. "Close enough."

I closed my eyes, took a deep breath in, and let it out.

I pressed the trigger.

Nothing happened.

I stood there, frozen and shaking, until Jemma reached over and gently pried the burner from my hand.

"Congratulations," she said quietly. "As of today, you're officially Mickey1."

THERE'S QUITE A crowd waiting for me by the main lock. Marshall is there, along with Dugan from Biology and a gaggle of Security goons. Berto and Nasha are standing off to one side. Berto's hunched over, his face just inches from hers. He says something, short and sharp. She looks away and shakes her head.

"Hey," I say. "What's going on?"

Marshall waves me over. "Take a look," he says, and gestures to the monitor over the lock. I look up. The outer door is sealed. There's a blackened, mostly man-shaped blob slumped in one corner.

"Shit." I look closer. What I'd taken for blackened metal is actually a hole almost two meters across in the floor of the lock. "Where's the decking?"

"Gone," says Dugan. "Something punched through while Gallaher there was waiting for the lock to cycle and started peeling it away."

"Gallaher? You mean that lump in the corner?"

"Yes," says Marshall. "That's him. We had to use the murder hole."

I can feel my jaw sag. "You vented plasma into the main lock? While one of our people was *in it*?"

"We did," Marshall says. "Gallaher was seriously wounded, in the process of bleeding out. The thing that ripped out the first section of decking sheared off most of his left leg in the process. The AI controlling perimeter security made the call, and I'm not inclined to second-guess it. We couldn't risk penetration into the dome."

I'm not sure what to say to that.

"It was creepers," says Berto. "At least two or three of them."

I shake my head. "How . . ."

"Apparently those mandibles are sharper than they look," he says. "I mean, I've seen them go through stuff before—"

"Stuff?" I say. "You mean like my skull?"

That gets me five seconds of awkward silence.

"Anyway," Dugan says, "I was surprised to find that we don't have any hard data on these things. I was able to call up a couple of descriptions in picket reports from Gomez and Adjaya, but that's pretty much it. That's why we called you down."

I look to Berto, then back to Dugan.

"Gomez says you've got some personal experience with these things," he says. "Says you've developed a bit of an obsession with them, in fact, and Commander Marshall tells me he's had you out observing them for the past few weeks. We need more than that. We need to figure out exactly what we're dealing with. If they start knocking holes in the dome, we're finished."

I glance over at Berto again. He won't meet my eyes.

"Personal experience?"

"Right," Marshall says. "Because they've eaten you."

"True enough," says Berto. "Mickey's an expert at getting eaten by creepers."

Berto and Nasha are both looking at me now. I roll my eyes.

"We just went over this. I don't remember anything about what happened to Six or Seven. I wouldn't even know it'd happened if Berto hadn't told me about it."

"You sure, Mickey?" Berto says. "This is important. You don't remember anything from last night?"

Berto stares me down. Nasha looks away.

"I just came out of the tank this morning. You know this, Berto."

Marshall's eyes narrow. "Is there something going on here that I need to be made aware of?"

Berto gives me one more dubious look, then shakes his head.

"No, sir. We're good. Mickey's right. As we discussed this morning, he hadn't uploaded in some time when he went down last night."

Marshall's not an idiot, but I guess he decides he's got bigger fish to fry. After giving Berto another long, hard stare, he says, "Whatever. Get geared up, all of you. Gomez and Adjaya, you'll be providing air cover. I want a complete sweep with ground-penetrating radar from the dome out to two thousand meters beyond the perimeter. I want to know exactly how many of these things are out there, and where they're located. I also want you loaded for bear. Make sure your missile tubes are full before you lift. Once we've accomplished what we need to accomplish and extracted our people, I want the entire field cleared of those things out to a kilometer at least." He pauses to look around. "The rest of you, be ready to step out of the auxiliary lock on foot in fifteen minutes. Dugan—if you're going to develop an understanding of what these things are and what they can do, you need to have a specimen in your lab." He grins, but the expression is more ghoulish than happy. "You gentlemen are going on a snipe hunt."

"YOU KNOW," I say, "I've done this before."

"Huh?"

Dugan looks up at me. He and I haven't interacted much since that first day on Himmel Station. I don't get seconded out to Biology often, and when I do it's mostly for things like cleaning the labs. He's strapping himself into combat armor at the moment, which under other circumstances would be kind of hilarious. For the right kind of guy, being half in and half out of a battle suit makes you look like a war god from one of the old stories. Dugan is not that kind of guy. He looks like a plucked chicken getting ready for a costume party.

"I said, I've done this before. You don't want that armor."

He looks around. The Security goons are already geared up. I've been trying to remember their names for the last ten minutes. The scowly bald guy is Robert something—whatever you do, don't call him Bob—and the shorter woman is Cat Chen. The third one I'm pretty sure is named Gillian, but I wouldn't swear to that one. They're clanking around the armory at the moment, making sure all their servos are working. This will be the first armored sortie we've attempted since landfall.

"Seems like that's a minority opinion," he says.

I shrug. "They're Security. They'd wear armor to bed at night if they could. Armor may make you feel like you're invincible, but those suits add almost a hundred kilos. That makes you too heavy for snowshoes, and you really want to be on top of the snow when we go out there. Slogging through a meter or more of loose powder is really, really unpleasant."

He looks me up and down. I'm bundled up pretty well, but strictly in cold-weather gear. He's got two burners in hip holsters. I'm carrying a linear accelerator. It's heavier than what he's bringing and a lot less versatile, and I'm pretty sure my sprained wrist is going to complain bitterly if I have to actually bring it to bear, but it's the only weapon I have any real training on—and anyway, ever since that last night on Himmel Station, I've had kind of an aversion to burners.

"I appreciate the advice," he says, "but I saw what those things in the lock did to Gallaher's leg. I'd like to have something a little more substantial than a snowsuit between them and me."

"You saw what they did to Gallaher. Did you see what they did to the decking?"

He's glaring now, looking back and forth between me and his right gauntlet, which he doesn't seem to be able to get to slip into the fitting on his sleeve.

"Let me see that," I say. He holds up his arm. I give the gauntlet a twist, and the connector latches.

"Thanks," he says. He flexes his hand, makes sure everything's hooked up, then reaches for his chest plate. "I get it," he says as he snaps that into place. "This is no big deal for you. But you've got to understand, Barnes—the rest of us don't get to just hit the reset button if we go down. Dead is dead for me. So, yeah, I'm wearing armor."

I smile. "Reset button, huh? That what you think a trip to the tank is?"

"Look," he says. "I'm not trying to start something here, but the fact is that you're an Expendable, and I'm not. Our incentives are different. I just want to go out there, collect our sample, and get back in here intact."

I lift the accelerator's strap over my head. I want it loose enough that I can bring the weapon to bear quickly, but tight enough that it's not banging against my back while I'm walking.

"I'm definitely not about to argue that point," I say. "The whole reset-button thing isn't as much fun as you apparently think it is."

My ocular pings.

<Command1>:Adjaya and Gomez are starting their sweep. Time to go.

I look around. The goons are clanking toward the lock. I seal up my rebreather. Dugan dogs his helmet, and we go.

THE LAST TIME anything native seriously opposed one of our landfalls was a bit under two hundred years ago, and maybe fifty lights spinward from here. The beachhead Command there probably gave the place a name, but if they did, they never let the rest of us know. These days, the planet is called Roanoke.

Roanoke is not what you'd call an ideal habitat. Its star is a red dwarf, and the planet itself is a tidally locked rock with almost no axial tilt, very little water, and a thirty-one-day orbital period. It's got a hot pole on one side, where the ambient temperature rarely drops below eighty C, a cold pole on the other side where it snows CO_2, and a more or less habitable strip of perpetual twilight circumscribing the planet in between that's maybe a thousand kilometers wide. Roanoke is an old world. Speculation is that it's harbored life for maybe seven billion years. And all that time, everything that's evolved there has been fighting for a toehold in that dry, wind-scoured, thousand-kilometer strip.

Apparently, bringing a few million liters of liquid water to a place like that is like bringing a giant sack of scrip to a shantytown, because the colony wasn't a week past landfall before things started coming after them. There were tiny biting things that came on the wind, burrowed into any exposed skin, and brought itching rashes, then pus-filled blisters, then sepsis, then death. There were things like sand-burrowing starfish with armor-piercing fangs. They injected a necrotizing venom that killed in minutes. There were insectile things half the size of a man that shot jets of concentrated sulfuric acid from glands in their heads. Most of the creatures on the planet seemed purpose-built to defeat the colony's defenses, and though it seems obvious to us now what was going on, as near as we can tell from the records their

Command transmitted before they went down, they never did figure it out.

Almost from day one, Command on Roanoke couldn't keep their people alive outside the main dome for more than an hour. They lost them in ones and twos, week after week, until finally, taboos be damned, they had to start making extra copies of their Expendable just to keep their berths filled.

They eventually did button the place up and try to hunker down and do some research into what was happening to them. By that time, though, something was reproducing inside the dome. Command tried a half dozen sterilization protocols, but whatever it was, it kept coming back. By the end, the entire colony was made up of copies. The central processor kept cranking them out until it ran out of amino acids.

One of the last of the Expendables to die got at least a glimmer of the truth, just before the end. Bio had released a phage tuned to take out one of the microorganisms that was tearing them up. A resistant strain showed up six hours later. The last words in his personal log, dictated as his innards were liquefying and pouring out of every orifice, were these: I am not paranoid. Someone here really is out to get me.

I'M THINKING ABOUT that guy, Jerrol-two-hundred-and-something, as we step out into the snow. The locals on Roanoke didn't ring any alarm bells with the colonists there because they weren't tool-users in the classic sense. They didn't produce any electromagnetic emissions, didn't have power plants or roads or cars or cities. Didn't even have agriculture, as far as we could tell. They were, as it turned out, crazy-good genetic engineers, though. Combine that with their extreme territoriality and xenophobia— pretty predictable, considering that they'd spent their entire evolutionary history fighting with each other and everything else on their crappy planet over a thin band of marginally habitable territory—and you got a bad outcome for the Roanoke beachhead.

I'm thinking about Jerrol, and I'm thinking about my gigantic tunnel-digging friend from last night. Everybody died on Roanoke because there were sentients there, and the colonists failed to notice them until it was too late. I'm wondering if somebody like me maybe had a run-in with one of the locals on Roanoke, identified it as a sentient, and then failed to report it in to Command.

A fair number of beachhead colonies fail for one reason or another. I'd really hate to have this one fail because of me.

THE LAST GLOW of sunset is fading on the horizon, and the first stars are already visible in the eastern sky. We're ten minutes out from the lock, maybe a half kilometer past the perimeter, and Dugan is conferring with Berto and Nasha over the comm about where best to find one creeper but not a hundred, when Cat clomps over to me. Back in the armory we were about the same height, but I'm standing on top of almost a meter of snow now, and she has to crane her neck to look up at me.

"Hey," she says. "What's with the LA? I thought we were all packing burners."

It takes me a second to realize that she's talking about my weapon. I don't really want to go into my Jemma-inspired aversion to burners at the moment. I don't know this person at all, and even after nine years, that story still feels a little raw.

"No reason," I say. "Just a feeling, really."

"A feeling, huh? That's a good way to pick an outfit for a first date, but it's a strange way to pick a weapon, isn't it?"

Okay. Apparently she's not going to let this go.

"My feeling, specifically, was that I don't think burners are likely to be effective against creepers."

"Oh. Speaking from personal experience?"

I shrug. I can't see her face through her mirrored visor, but there's definitely a hint of worry in her voice.

"Not really. But when we were in the armory, I asked myself what I'd usually pick out for something like this."

She cocks her head to one side. "Well?"

"A burner. Definitely a burner. The max rate of fire on this thing I'm carrying is one round per second, and it's heavy as shit. I mean, not nearly as heavy as all that stupid armor, but still."

"I don't get it."

I smile, though she can't see it behind my rebreather. "Doing what I usually do has gotten me taken down by these things twice now. So, this time I did the opposite."

She nods. "Got it. That's very Zen of you, Barnes."

"Well, I do keep getting reincarnated."

"True," she says. "Working your way toward Nirvana, right?"

This seems like a weird time for banter, but okay. I shake my head. "I don't think so. I keep expecting to come back as a tapeworm or something."

"But every time, you wake up as you. Maybe Mickey Barnes is as low as you can go, karmically speaking."

I look around. Nothing important seems to be happening.

"Yeah," I say. "I guess so."

Dugan is standing almost waist-deep in the snow twenty meters or so away, still jawing with Berto. I could tell him where he can find plenty of creepers—or at least one really big one—but I'm guessing that wouldn't go over well with anyone. I look up. It's a beautiful night, by Niflheim standards. The sky is clear and deep and black. There's enough light bleeding off from the dome to make it so that only a few stars are visible, but the ones that are there are hard, bright bits of silver.

"You know," Cat says, "I don't think we've ever really talked before, have we?"

I look back down at her. She's watching Dugan, one hand on her burner.

"No," I say. "Not that I remember, anyway."

"That's weird, isn't it? Have you been avoiding me?"

I'm about to tell her that, no, it's not weird that we've never spoken, because half the people on the *Drakkar* thought I was some kind of abomination, and half the rest just found me generally creepy, and so for the past nine years I've never really reached out to anybody who didn't reach out to me first—which she apparently never did. Before I can get into all that, though, the whine of gravitics rises and then dies away as Nasha sweeps by, maybe sixty meters overhead.

"Come on," Dugan says over the comm. "We're moving."

We trudge north, away from the dome and toward the place where I emerged from the tunnels this morning. What would Dugan do if my gigantic friend popped up out of the snow in front of him?

"Something funny?" Cat asks.

"Not really," I say. "I was just thinking of something."

"Tell me," she says. "I'm bored."

I can't tell her, of course. I also can't tell her that I can't tell her, because then I'd have to tell her *why* I can't tell her. I don't have to figure out where I'm going with that one, though, because just then Dugan starts yelling. Yelling, and dancing.

"Hey," Cat says. "What the . . ."

That's when Dugan lifts his right leg up out of the snow, and I see that it's wrapped in creeper. There are divots in the armor where the thing's pointy little feet are dug in, and its mandibles are working on the seam at the back of his knee.

Things happen quickly now. The other two goons, who have been flanking Dugan for the past ten minutes, turn their burners on his leg. He seems to be encouraging them at first, but then the armor starts glowing and the creeper is still chewing and its legs dig deeper and deeper into the softening armor and as a gout of live steam rises up from the snow to hide them, Dugan's yelling turns into screaming turns into a wordless shriek. I spin half around. Maybe thirty meters off, a hunk of gray granite juts out of the snow. I start running.

Running in snowshoes is not efficient, and it is not fun. I haven't gone three steps before I stumble and fall face-first into the snow. I'm flailing, expecting every second to feel a creeper's mandibles sinking into the back of my neck, when a powered gauntlet grabs me by the arm and hauls me to my feet.

"Come on," Cat says. "Move!"

She gives me a shove in the back, and I almost fall again before stumbling forward. I can hear Cat slogging after me, and farther away the cursing and then screaming of the other two goons. I risk a glance back. The steam is being carried away on a stiff north wind. Dugan is gone—dragged under the snow, I guess. The two from Security are still on their feet, but they're wearing a couple of creepers each, and I'm guessing that won't last long.

I scramble up onto the rock, reach over my shoulder for the accelerator, and bring it to bear, wincing as my left hand takes the weight of the barrel. A second later, Cat climbs up beside me. We're on a granite island maybe three meters across, sticking up a half meter or so above the snow. A creeper pokes its head up, almost close enough for me to touch. I aim and fire. The kick of the accelerator pushes me back into Cat, and in the same instant the creeper's first three segments explode into a hail of shrapnel.

"Shit," Cat says. "Zen for the win, huh?"

The other Security goons are down now, though I think I can still see some thrashing going on under the snow. I open my mouth to speak, but then a rising screech of gravitics announces Berto's arrival. Twin spotlights illuminate first us, then the place where Dugan and the others went down.

"Have you got a sample?" Berto asks over the comm.

"Part of one."

I hop down off the rock and grab what's left of the creeper. Berto's grapple is already descending. I climb back up and hand the creeper to Cat, then latch the grapple to her armor. She wraps one arm around my chest, and we ascend. When I look down a few seconds later, the top of the rock is swarming with creepers. We're barely into Berto's cargo bay when Nasha comes screaming in, low and fast, first two missiles already loosed. The bay door slams, and we ride the first wave of expanding plasma up and away.

GETTING SENT ON near-suicide missions like Marshall's snipe hunt is pretty much routine for me at this point. Getting rescued, on the other hand, is not. That part is a little disorienting. Even before she staged my mock execution, Jemma made sure I was one hundred percent clear on what to expect in situations like that, and it definitely wasn't Berto riding in like my guardian angel and spiriting me away.

I sometimes wonder if maybe Jemma didn't do *too* good a job of letting me know exactly what being an Expendable was about. After the *Drakkar* had slipped her moorings and boosted out of orbit around Midgard, I spent the first few weeks of the journey wandering around the corridors in a funk, waiting morosely for one of the things she had prepped me for to happen, waiting to be told to climb into the engines or step out an air lock or stick my head in a blender to see whether the blades were sharp enough.

For a long time, though, none of those things happened. That ship represented a huge fraction of Midgard's accumulated wealth, and the systems architects had put a fair amount of effort into making as certain as possible that she'd get where she was going without exploding—and despite my worst expectations, nobody seemed to be particularly interested in killing me just for fun.

The longer we went without any disasters, and the more I thought about what we were actually doing, the more I started to expect that I might actually reach Niflheim without ever having to go through the tank. I mean, the one thing everyone knows about interstellar travel is that it's boring, right? And, especially once you're finished with the boost phase, which is when the engines are working hard and the ship's frame is under stress and you'd think anything that's likely to break is going to do it, it really is. The cruise phase of a colony mission, as it turns out, is in fact dull as dirt.

Until it isn't, anyway.

The last thing I remember about life in the body I was born with is a technician slipping the upload helmet over my head as my arms and legs spasmed and blood seeped out of my mouth and nose and pooled under my blistering skin. We were a bit more than a year out from Midgard by then. We'd gotten through first boost, pushed through our sun's heliopause at sub-relativistic speed, cranked the engines back up for second boost, and finally settled in at a hair under point-nine c for the long glide to Niflheim.

Life on the *Drakkar* was easy, for the most part. As far as the actual ship's crew were concerned, the bulk of the colonists were basically baggage during transit. Because I wasn't attached to any particular branch, I was even more so. I was supposed to be doing two hours of training per day, rotating among branches so that I could serve as a stopgap for any of them as the need arose, but a lot of the folks who should have been training me thought I was spooky, and some of the others, like the engineers, were actually busy doing their jobs and didn't have time to spare for training someone with zero technical expertise, so it mostly worked out to more like two hours a week. Outside of that I fed myself, took naps, and hung around the common areas with Berto playing puzzle games on our tablets. Throw in some gravity, and it wouldn't have been that different from my life on Midgard.

As I was about to be reminded, though, we weren't on Midgard. We were moving through interstellar space at two hundred and seventy million meters per second—and at those sorts of speeds, high-energy physics takes over from Mr. Newton, and things get wacky.

Space, as Jemma carefully explained to me, is not as empty as you might think. Any given cubic meter of what we think of as hard vacuum actually contains on the order of a hundred thousand hydrogen atoms, for instance. Hydrogen atoms are benign at rest, but at point-nine c they're dangerous projectiles. The *Drakkar* had a field generator in her nose that shunted them aside, and turned them into a continuous stream of cosmic rays just above the surface of the hull as we plowed through the interstellar medium—so, not a problem as long as you stayed inside, which everyone on the ship other than possibly me was definitely going to do for the duration.

Interstellar space also contains the occasional dust grain—only about one in every million cubic meters, but every square meter of the ship's surface area was passing through two hundred and seventy million cubic meters of space every second, so we bumped into those on a pretty regular basis as well. The vast majority of those grains carried enough net charge to get funneled along the surface and away by our field generator. Some of them didn't, which produced a continuous patter of tiny explosions against the nose cone. The ship was designed to withstand that, though. The armor on the nose was ablative, and thick enough to survive twenty years or more of normal wear and tear.

The armor was not, however, designed to withstand the impact of anything much bigger than a dust grain.

In fairness to the folks who put the *Drakkar* together, things bigger than that are pretty rare once you're past the heliopause, and there's no such thing as armor thick enough to protect you from an actual macro object. A rock the size of my head carries a hundred times the energy of a fusion bomb at *Drakkar*'s cruising speed.

Luckily, the thing that hit us wasn't quite that big.

We don't know what, exactly, the object was, obviously. It got reduced to its component quarks and gluons on impact. We know it massed between fifteen and twenty grams, though. One of the engineers calculated that based on the volume of armor that it vaporized, and the amount of kinetic energy the ship gave up on impact.

The jolt wasn't trivial, by the way. We were in free fall, so most things were reasonably well secured, but anything that wasn't— including a fair number of the crew—went flying into the forward bulkheads. There were a couple of broken arms, and one significant concussion. I clipped the edge of a table as I fell, and wound up spraining an ankle.

Nobody cared about any of that. There was a hole in the nose cone and one of the field generation modules was gone. Twenty percent of the interior volume of the ship was suddenly flooded with hard radiation.

It was my time to shine.

The summons came from Maggie Ling, who was the head of Systems Engineering during transit. She met me in the machine shop, which was the nearest safe compartment to the nose cone access hatch. Two of her people stuffed me into a vacuum suit while she explained exactly what she needed me to do.

"We think the power coupling is shot," she said. "We're not

sure, though, and we don't have time to screw around, so you're replacing the entire unit." Another of the engineers had just finished unpacking a half-meter-square silver cube from a storage crate. It had two floating connector cables on one side, and two maneuvering handles on the other. "When you're done with that, get the old unit back here if you can."

"If I can?"

"Yeah," she said. "Before you die, right? That compartment is open to space at the moment. Until you can get this unit running, you'll be absorbing a lethal full-body radiation dose every three-point-five seconds."

I must have given her a look then, because she rolled her eyes.

"Don't worry. That doesn't mean you're going to die the minute you go through the hatch. The human body takes a surprisingly long time to actually shut down, even after it's picked up many times a fatal dose. As long as you don't take a direct hit from a grain, you should have plenty of time to upload before you go, and we've already got your next instantiation cooking in the tank."

There were a bunch of things in that short statement that I wanted to argue with. Start with the fact that I was a lot more concerned about the dying part than about the specific timing of it, or whether I'd be able to upload before that happened, and follow that up with her assumption that I was going to do this despite the fact that nobody had actually asked me.

The fact was, though . . . she was right. I was doing this. Jemma had gone over the importance of the field generator with me in painful detail, and I was perfectly clear on how boned we were until that unit was replaced.

Once they'd finished securing my helmet, I very, very carefully hefted the generator and guided it over toward the portable air lock they'd rigged over the access hatch.

"Did I mention we're in a bit of a hurry?" Maggie asked over the comm. I grunted a reply, but I didn't move any faster. Heavy things don't have weight in free fall, but they still have mass, and it's really easy to smash things up if you get them moving too quickly. Once I was inside the lock, they sealed the outer door behind me, and my suit went taut as they evacuated the chamber. When the whistle of escaping air had completely died away, the hatch slid open.

The field generator was an array of six cubes, each exactly like the one I was carrying. I could see immediately which one was the problem. The unit nearest me as I entered the chamber had a black-rimmed hole maybe two or three centimeters wide punched straight through the top. I looked up. There was a slightly larger hole in the roof of the chamber. A beam of bluish light passed through it, and illuminated the top of the wrecked unit like a spotlight.

It was just about then that my skin started burning.

It wasn't too bad at first. As Maggie and Jemma had said, the human body is surprisingly slow to react to acute radiation poisoning. I pulled the cables from the old unit, opened the docking latches, and got it up and out without any real trouble. When I was trying to get the new unit positioned, though, my head must have passed through that beam of light.

About ten seconds later, I was blind.

The skin on my hands was bubbling up by then, and I didn't have much sense of touch left. The unit was latched down, and I'd managed to get the first docking cable engaged—but when I moved to the second one, I couldn't figure out where the port was. I groped around for a few seconds, cable in hand, increasingly panicked, before Maggie spoke in my ear.

"Barnes? You okay?"

I tried to say *no,* but my tongue was too swollen to make the sounds, and all that came out was a moan.

"Stop," she said. "Don't yank on the cable."

I stopped, or tried to. My body was shaking too badly to really hold still.

"Your helmet camera is still functioning for the moment. Try to position it so that I can see what you're doing."

I felt for the edge of the unit, then bowed my head toward where I thought the connector should go.

"Okay," Maggie said. "Hold the camera there. Now move the connector to your left. Approximately ten centimeters."

I slid the connector across the floor.

"Good," Maggie said. "Now forward about three.

"Right one.

"Back one.

"Press."

I felt a click as the connector snapped into place.

"Perfect," Maggie said. "Field is reestablished. Good job, Barnes. Try to relax now. We'll get somebody in there to retrieve you."

It's surprisingly difficult to relax when your body is burning from the inside out. If I could have just popped the seals on my helmet and decompressed then, I would have done it, but my hands were worse than useless, my fingers too swollen to bend. So I floated there, shaking and moaning and grinding my teeth, and waited for someone to pull me back into the world.

I understand why they forced me to upload before they let me die. Jemma covered that too. Knowledge and experience gained during a critical situation is valuable, and that can't be permitted to die with one particular instantiation of me.

Some things, though, just really need to be forgotten.

The situation was slightly less critical by the time I came out of the tank as Mickey2. The field generator was functioning, and conditions inside the *Drakkar* were basically back to normal—at least if you set aside the thirty-four people who were now suffering from various degrees of radiation poisoning because they'd been in the wrong parts of the ship when the field went down. We still had a hole in our armor, though, and all it would have taken was a stray grain in the right spot to put us right back where we'd been. So, as soon as I was conscious and functioning, Maggie and her people crammed me into another vacuum suit and sent me out onto the hull with a tank full of high-density emergency patch nanites, and five minutes' worth of direction on how to use them.

The highest intensity in the stream of protons being channeled along the hull was about two meters off the surface. Maggie told me that if I stayed close to the hull and was lucky enough to avoid getting clipped by a grain, I might even keep my exposure low enough to survive. So, I tried. Rather than just giving me force locks for my boots, like Jemma and I wore when we hiked out over Midgard, Maggie had them strap smaller attractors to my palms and knees. I went out through the forward air lock, and crawled the hundred meters or so to the impact point.

At first I thought I might be okay. As I approached the nose, though, the proton stream closed in. I started seeing flashes of light with maybe twenty meters to go, and by the time I reached the hole, my vision was blurring and my mouth tasted of iron. I pulled the nanite tank from my back, unlimbered the applicator, and pressed the trigger.

The nanites came out in a thick, sticky stream. They clung to the ragged walls of the hole, and even as I was still dispensing them they started to knit themselves together into the same hyper-dense material as the surrounding armor.

It took almost twenty minutes to empty the tank. When it was done, there was a mound of goo where the hole had been. Over the next few minutes, it flattened and smoothed itself until it would have taken an electron microscope to tell the difference between the patch and the original armor.

I only know any of this because when I came out of the tank as Mickey3 the next morning, the first thing they made me do was watch the video feed from my suit camera and listen to the running narrative I'd kept up right until the point when, halfway back to the air lock, I stopped moving, popped the seals at my collar, and showed my naked face to the universe.

"WELL," BERTO SAYS from the cockpit, "that could have gone better."

Cat shoots him a murderous glance. Berto's never been much for sensitivity.

"Three people just died," I say.

"Yeah," Berto says. "I saw. What the hell happened down there? It looked like Security turned their burners on Dugan?"

"They were trying to save him," Cat says.

"Hell of a way to do it," Berto says as we bank over the main dome and slow to a hover over the landing pad. "Even combat armor won't stand up to a burner set to full power for long. What were they thinking?"

I glance over at Cat. Her hands are clenched into fists.

"They were thinking Dugan had two creepers wrapped around his leg," she says. "And not for nothing, but those were my friends down there, asshole. Also not for nothing, maybe if you'd warned us that we were standing on top of a nest of those fucking things, the whole sortie would have gone a little better, huh?"

Berto glances back from the cockpit as we settle down onto

the pad. I'm slightly surprised to see that he actually looks embarrassed.

"Sorry," he says. "No disrespect intended."

"Yeah, well," Cat says. "Disrespect taken."

Berto powers the lifter down, then starts working through his shutdown checklist. I can feel my weight settle a little more firmly into the padding of my jump seat as the gravitic field dissipates.

"I really am sorry about what happened out there," Berto says. "I would have warned you if I could have. I don't know where those things came from, but they weren't just moving under the snow. There was nothing on my radar the last time I passed over you, and that was no more than a minute before the attack."

"Whatever," Cat says. I can't see her face through her visor, but I can hear the scowl in her voice.

"Anyway," Berto says, "mission accomplished, right?" As Cat and I unbuckle, he climbs out of his seat and comes back to stand over us. What's left of the creeper lies on the floor of the cabin. Berto nudges it with the toe of one boot. Two of its legs spasm, and he almost trips himself yanking his foot back. "Shit!" He regains his balance, grimaces, then steps forward again and crouches down between us. The carcass is vibrating. He touches the carapace with one finger, but this time it doesn't react. "Huh," he says. "I hope this turns out to've been worth it."

"YOU'RE GOING TO need to help me out here," Marshall says. "Because I'm having a lot of trouble understanding how we lost three people in the last two hours—four, if you count Gallaher, and five if you count Torricelli—and you weren't one of them."

Cat shifts uncomfortably in her seat next to me. Marshall leans forward, elbows on his desk. He doesn't look like he's trying to decide whether to kill me or not. He looks like he's trying to settle on the method.

"You're right, sir," I say. "I apologize for surviving. I'll try to do better next time."

That brings him to his feet. "Don't give me that shit, Barnes! You're an Expendable! You're not supposed to be worried about surviving!"

He sits back down slowly, while I wipe his spittle from my forehead.

"Now," he says, "I want you to explain to me, clearly and concisely, why you chose to save your own ass out there rather than rendering aid to Mr. Dugan. Give this some thought, Barnes, because if I don't find your answer convincing, I'm going to personally shove you down the corpse hole balls-first."

"Sir—" Cat says.

"Shut up, Chen. I'll deal with you when I'm done with him."

They're both looking at me now, Cat with a mixture of pity and concern, Marshall with the same basic expression a hawk might give to a field mouse.

"Well," I begin, then hesitate. I was going to say something about how it's all well and good to say I shouldn't be worried about surviving when he's sitting safe and sound in the same body he was born with, while I'm getting irradiated or eaten or dissolved every six weeks, but looking at his face, I suddenly realize that he might be serious about the whole corpse hole thing. I begin again.

"Well, sir, we were sent out there for a reason. You ordered us to retrieve a creeper. Given what happened to Torricelli and Gallaher, we were all very much aware that this was a hazardous sortie, but you decided that we should attempt it anyway. Therefore, I concluded that doing what we were sent out there to do was our first priority. By the time we realized what was happening to Mr. Dugan, it was my judgment that there was nothing we could have done to help him. Therefore, I decided to put my efforts to accomplishing the mission—which, I will note, I succeeded in doing."

Marshall stares at me for what feels like a very long time. "So what you're saying," he says, "is that what I saw on Gomez's video feed was not in fact you running for your life in abject terror, but rather you calmly doing what was necessary to further the mission and protect the colony. Is that correct?"

I look at Cat. She shrugs.

"Uh . . . yes?"

The silence stretches on for a long five seconds. Cat opens her mouth to speak, but Marshall silences her with a glance.

"Did you know, prior to leaving the dome, that our burners would be ineffective against those things?"

"No," I say. "Not for sure."

"Then why did you choose to carry an accelerator?"

"Primarily because I'm better trained in the use of an accelerator than in the use of a burner, sir. Also, I'm aware that I was carrying a burner on two other occasions when I encountered creepers, and that I did not survive either of those missions. So, I thought this time it might be wise to change tactics."

Marshall's eyebrows come together at the bridge of his nose, and his mouth shrinks down into a thin, hard line. I risk a glance over at Cat. She's staring straight ahead. Marshall turns his attention to her.

"What about you, Chen? Can you explain your actions? You were out there to protect Mr. Dugan, were you not?"

"Yes, sir," she says. "I was."

"And you abandoned him because . . ."

"I abandoned him because I could see what was happening, sir. The other two Security officers were my friends. If I had believed that I could do anything to help them, I would have done it. But the fact is, our weapons were not useful, and I couldn't see any point in feeding myself to those things along with Mr. Dugan."

"Barnes's weapon was useful. You could have commandeered it."

"I could have," she says, "but I couldn't have done anything useful with it. A linear accelerator isn't a precision weapon, sir. I could have blown Mr. Dugan's leg off, but I couldn't have saved him."

Marshall leans back from his desk and runs his hands back through his brush-cut salt-and-pepper hair.

"Look," he says. "We began this expedition with one hundred and ninety-eight people. We made landfall with one hundred and eighty, and we are now down to one hundred and seventy-five. From a population standpoint, we are fast approaching the limit of viability for a beachhead colony. Because of this, I unfortunately can't actually shove either one of you down the corpse hole at this time, or even punish you in any meaningful way, much though I might like to do so.

"Barnes, I have a strong suspicion that you know more about those things out there than you're telling us. If this is true, I can only ask you to think very carefully about what you're doing, because if this colony goes down, you will wind up spending your last days like that poor sick bastard on Roanoke, in the company of a whole shitload of Mickey Barneses—which, I can tell you from my experience with just one of you, would be absolutely unbearable.

"Chen, I really don't know what to make of you at this point. I'm beginning to suspect that you may have had some preexisting relationship with Barnes, which you should have disclosed prior to the sortie. In the future, please remember that you need to let Command know if the possibility exists that personal issues may interfere with the performance of your mission."

Cat opens her mouth to speak, but Marshall cuts her off again with a slash of one hand.

"I don't want to hear it," he says. "I just want you to think very carefully about who you choose to associate with in the future."

He looks at me, then Cat, then back at me. "That's all," he says. "Go. We'll let you know when you're needed again."

"So," Cat says. "That was fun."

We're in the cafeteria, catching a late-shift dinner. There are at least thirty people here, gathered in groups of three or four, leaning over their tables, heads close together, talking in low voices. Five deaths in one day is a scary thing on a beachhead colony, and we're mostly engaged in the ancient human custom of telling one another what idiots the recently deceased were, in order to convince ourselves that what happened to them can't possibly happen to us.

"Yeah," I say. "He didn't actually murder us. I call that a win."

That gets a smile. Cat's much prettier in a jumpsuit than she was in battle gear. Her face is soft and heart-shaped, and her hair is thick and black and pulled back into a shoulder-length ponytail. She's picking at a plate of roasted tomatoes and a stringy-looking rabbit haunch. I'm working my way through a hundred-kcal half-full mug of cycler paste. I know I promised Eight the rest of our ration for the day, but I just nearly died while he was napping. That has to count for something, right?

"So," I say. "Marshall thinks we're sexing, huh?"

Cat's face hardens into a scowl. "Marshall can fuck himself."

"Wow," I say. "That's pretty harsh. Don't want anyone thinking that you're associating with the Expendable, huh?"

She shakes her head. "Nah. I'm not a Natalist or anything. As far as I'm concerned, you're no different from any of the other weirdos who signed up for this trip. What I don't like is the insinuation that I didn't do my job because my *hormones* got in the way. I mean, I didn't hear him giving you any shit about that, right?"

"I didn't . . ." I trail off, because I was about to say *I didn't think he meant it that way,* and it's just occurred to me that yeah, he probably did.

"You didn't what?"

"Nothing," I say. "You're one hundred percent right. Fuck that guy."

"Amen," she says, and raises her water cup to me. "Fuck that guy."

I tap my mug to her cup, and we drink.

While she's distracted with that, I snatch a tomato from her tray and cram it into my mouth before she can react.

"Hey," she growls, then reaches across the table and punches my shoulder hard enough to leave a bruise. "No screwing around, Barnes. You touch my food again and I'll break your arm."

"Sorry," I say, and push my mug of paste toward her. "You can have some of mine if you want."

She scowls again and pushes it back. "Thanks, I'm good. If you want a tomato, why don't you just go get one? Did you seriously eat through your entire day's rations before the sortie?"

"Yeah," I say. "Pretty much. I've had a rough few days."

"Oh," she says. "Right. I forgot you went down last night. You're fresh out of the tank, huh?" She takes a bite, chews, and swallows. "What's that like?"

"What, coming out of the tank?"

She nods, picks up the rabbit bone, and gnaws at a bit of meat left around the joint. "Yeah. I've always wondered what it's like to wake up and know that you just died, that the body you're in was a bunch of protein paste in the bio-cycler a few hours before. How does that feel?"

"Well," I say, "you're not conscious in the tank. You wake up in your bed. You're a little disoriented and a lot hungover, and you can't remember how you got there. You think maybe you were out drinking the night before, except that you can't remember that either. The last thing you remember is plugging in to upload."

She leans back and nods. "Right. That's when you realize."

"Yeah, that's it. I've done it seven times now, and it's a kick in the crotch every time."

She gives me a sympathetic smile, but then her eyes focus over my left shoulder and the smile fades. I turn my head to see Nasha standing behind me, arms folded across her chest.

"Hey," she says. "How'd it go with Command?"

I slide over to make room for her. She steps over the bench and sits.

"Good," I say. "Well, more like adequate, I guess. Marshall threatened to cram me down the corpse hole, but he didn't actually do it."

Nasha grimaces. "Is that even a threat for you? After the shit that bastard did to you when we first made landfall, why would he think that would scare you?"

Cat looks at Nasha, then back at me. "Well," she says. "He did threaten to put him through balls-first."

Nasha shakes her head, and moves her hand to the small of my back. "Sister, you have no idea what this man has been through."

"You're talking about the medical stuff?"

"Yeah," Nasha says. "I'm talking about the medical stuff."

Cat looks away then, and goes back to picking at her rabbit bone. I nudge Nasha. Cat's had a rough go. She doesn't need to catch shade right now. Nasha sighs.

"Anyway," she says, "I'm sorry about what happened to Gillian and Rob out there. I know you guys were tight."

"Thanks," Cat says. "I already asked Gomez this, but . . . did you guys pick up anything before those things hit us? I mean, they couldn't have just materialized out of nothing, right?"

Nasha shakes her head. "Nope. Nothing. I was running visible, infrared, and ground-penetrating radar, and I swear you guys were one hundred percent clear the last time I passed over."

"Yeah," Cat says. "That's the same thing Gomez said. Between the two of you, we couldn't have been exposed for more than thirty seconds at a time. It doesn't make sense, does it?"

"I don't know," Nasha says. "They came at the main lock from underneath, right? GPR can't see through granite. Maybe they're miners. Hell, maybe they've got tunnels running straight up under us right now."

Cat glances down at her feet. "Thanks, Nasha. I hate that."

Nasha grins. "Lucky thing we've all got top-level racks, right?"

"Yeah," Cat says. "Lucky." She pokes halfheartedly at the last scraps of tomato skin on her tray, then looks over at me. "So you two have been together forever, right? Since Midgard?"

I look at Nasha. She shrugs.

"Almost. When he's not getting eaten or set on fire or crushed by falling storage bins, anyway. Why? You want a crack at him?"

"Doubtful," Cat says. "Why? Would it be worth the trouble?"

Nasha glances over at me. "Maybe. Depends on what you're into, I guess."

I can feel my face redden as they both burst out laughing.

"Just kidding," Nasha says, and wraps one arm around my shoulder. "This one's mine. You touch him, and I'll gut you like a fish."

Cat raises both hands in surrender. "Oh, no worries," she says. "His tomato-stealing ass is all yours. I was just leaving, actually."

She pushes back from the table and gathers her things. When she's gone, Nasha leans her forehead against mine and cups my cheek in one hand.

"Just so you know," she says, "she's not the only one I'd be gutting."

She kisses me quickly, gets to her feet, and goes.

I GET BACK to my rack to find Eight sitting in my chair, at my desk, reading something on my tablet. He shuts it down when he hears me enter. He's taken the pressure wrap off of his unsprained wrist.

"Hey," he says without looking up. "How'd it go?"

"Great," I say. "We're five corpses closer to getting you a berth of your own."

"Huh." He puts the tablet into the desk drawer, stands, and stretches. "Were we always a sociopath, or is this another one of your post-upload innovations?"

"Really? Were we always a sociopath?"

He grins. "Sorry. Pronouns weren't really designed for this situation, were they?"

"No," I say. "I guess not. And in answer to your question, no, we are not a sociopath. What we are is really, really hungry."

Eight barks out a humorless laugh. "Oh no," he says. "I don't want to hear anything from you about hungry. I just came out of the tank, remember? Try doing that on nothing but cycler paste."

"About that," I say, "I just used a hundred kcal. You've only got two hundred left now. Sorry."

His face hardens. "So much for being a good guy, huh?"

I shake my head. "Don't, Eight. I just almost got killed while you were napping. That's got to count for something."

"I may not have mentioned this," he says, "but I am literally starving to death, Seven."

He's right, of course. Six and I both bitched incessantly about the rations when we came out, and we were eating like kings compared to what Eight is getting. I peel out of my shirt and drop it on the floor, sit down on the bed and start unlacing my boots. Eight sits down next to me.

"Anyway," he says, "what's going on out there? The feed just says four accidental deaths and one gone missing, all outside the dome. How does that happen?"

I finish with the boots, pull them off, and lie back on the bed. "Well," I say. "First, they weren't all outside, strictly speaking. One was in the main lock, which by the way is no longer in service, since they just used the murder hole."

That hangs in the air for a long, awkward moment.

"The murder hole," Eight says finally. "They used it on what?"

I fold my hands behind my head and close my eyes. "Creepers."

Eight laughs, with a little more warmth this time. "Okay. Got it. You're shitting me. Really, what happened?"

"Really, they vented plasma into the lock to kill creepers that had breached the decking, and roasted a mostly dead Security goon named Gallaher in the process."

"Creepers are animals, Seven. You don't use live plasma to kill an animal."

"I don't think you're hearing me," I say. "*They breached the deck.*"

"By 'breached' you mean . . ."

"I mean they cut directly through the decking and started peeling it away."

"Peeling it away? You mean they . . . took it?"

I shrug. "Seems like it. This planet is metal-poor, you know. Maybe they need it for something."

"Huh." He scratches the top of his head. "Scoot over."

I slide over to make room for him, and he lies down next to me. This still feels weird, but there's been so much weirdness in my life in the past twenty-four hours that it barely registers.

"It's not like anybody thought they were harmless," Eight

says, "but it's a little hard to swallow an animal being able to rip through the ship's decking, isn't it?"

"You're not wrong." I'm about to go on, but I have to stop to yawn. I haven't slept except in two-hour stretches since the night before last. "I didn't see the bit with the decking, to be honest, but I saw the hole in the floor of the main lock. I also saw a bunch of creepers take down two fully armored goons and one very frightened biologist. It was not pretty."

"You're saying you saw creepers bite through ten-mil fiber armor?"

"Well," I say, "not that specifically. I saw them crawling around on ten-mil fiber armor, and I saw the guys wearing the armor go down. The actual biting-through-armor part was pretty strongly implied, though."

Eight rises up on one elbow and leans over me. "That doesn't make sense. Species don't evolve abilities that don't have uses in their environment. Why would an ice worm evolve the ability to bite through armor designed to stop a ten-gram LA slug?"

"That's an excellent question," I say, and yawn again. "I will definitely give you a good answer for it when I wake up."

Eight keeps talking, but his words slur into a dull background hum. The last conscious thing I remember is the bed shifting slightly as he stands.

ALMOST EVERY NIGHT for the past few weeks, I've had the same recurring . . . dream? No, more like a vision, I guess. It always comes just when I'm drifting off, or just when I'm waking. This is one reason why I haven't been uploading. I'm a little concerned that I might have suffered some kind of glitch during the regen process. If I did, I don't want to inject any of it into my personality record.

More importantly, I don't want anyone in psych to notice, and suggest that maybe they ought to scrap me and try again.

In the dream I'm back on Midgard, out in the woods that run along the crest of the Ullr Mountains. There's a trail there, eight hundred kilometers of untouched wilderness filled with waterfalls, hundred-kilometer vistas, and trees that have been growing since the original terraformers seeded the place three hundred years ago. I've walked it end-to-end four times. There's a lot of empty space on Midgard, but those mountains are the emptiest place on a mostly empty planet. In all the time I spent out there, I don't think I saw more than two or three other human beings.

I'm camped for the night, sitting on a log in front of a little fire, staring into the flames. So far, so good, right? Maybe I'm just homesick. But then I hear a noise, like someone clearing his throat. I look up, and there's this giant caterpillar sitting across the fire from me.

I know I should be freaking out right now, but I'm not. That's the part of the whole experience that's most like an actual dream.

The caterpillar and I talk—or try to, anyway. His mouth moves, and sounds come out that sound like words, but I can't make any sense of them. I tell him to stop, to slow down, that if he would just speak a little more clearly I could understand what he's saying. He doesn't, though. He just keeps going, until the listening makes my head start to ache. I look into the fire. It's running backward, unburning the pile of sticks it's feeding on and sucking smoke back out of the air. When I look up again, the caterpillar is fading, becoming less and less substantial, until only the smile remains.

Eventually even the smile disappears, and as it does I slide from this half world into a real dream, one I've had on and off for years. I'm Mickey2, out on the hull of the *Drakkar* again, crawling back toward the forward lock as my skin sloughs away and my blood begins seeping from ruptured vessels, covering me like fever sweat and draining into my mouth, my throat, my lungs.

I stop, and reach for the clasps at my neck. My fingers are like sausages now, swelling and splitting, but somehow I manage to fumble one clasp open, then the other. My helmet flies away, and hard vacuum sucks everything out of me.

Air.

Blood.

Shit.

Everything.

I should be dead now, but I'm not, and I can't understand why.

I open my cracked mouth and pull in a lungful of nothing. Before I can use it to scream, though, I snap awake, wide-eyed and sweating in the coal-black dark.